"So, teach me.

"Take me on for a week. Show me the ropes."
Rainer grinned at Jordan, as though he'd offered
the perfect solution.

"Ha! Not in a month of Sundays," she said, amused
despite herself. "Not in a million years. Not even
for a million bucks."

"Well, I can't go as high as a million, but how about
a hundred dollars?" Rainer offered.

"I laugh in your face."

"Five."

"Forget—"

"One thousand and you've got a deal," Cletus
interjected out of the blue.

"Done!" Rainer cried triumphantly. "I work for you
one week and—"

"And you pay us a thousand dollars," Jordan said in
a dry voice. "I wish all our employees were
so reasonable."

Day Leclaire knows all about the Seattle-based produce market described in her book, *In the Market*. She and her husband used to own it! Though what happens at Cornucopia is fictitious, she admits that more than one tomato battle *did* leave her store a little the worse for wear!

Books by Day Leclaire

HARLEQUIN ROMANCE
3028—JINXED
3139—WHERE THERE'S A WILL

IN THE MARKET
Day Leclaire

Harlequin Books

TORONTO • NEW YORK • LONDON
AMSTERDAM • PARIS • SYDNEY • HAMBURG
STOCKHOLM • ATHENS • TOKYO • MILAN

ISBN 0-373-03183-1

Harlequin Romance first edition March 1992

To my husband, Frank,
without whom this story would be impossible.

and

To Keith L. Andre,
who makes a great Viking role model.

and finally,

To my sister, Diane,
for loaning me her Viking husband.
Thanks!

IN THE MARKET

CHAPTER ONE

RAINER THORSEN RUBBED a hand across his squared jaw and shifted impatiently. He didn't like this—this endless waiting. Nor did he like standing around, biding his time and accomplishing nothing.

Everyone else moved with purpose, and normally he did, too. But this wholesale produce market wasn't his home turf. His retail operation utilized other wholesalers. As much as he wanted to grab a cart and help out the busy salesmen racing back and forth filling orders, he couldn't. His presence here served a different objective altogether.

Even so, hanging around a loading dock in downtown Seattle, staring at a woman—no matter how attractive—had him as near to crazy as he cared to get. It simply wasn't his style. *Action*—now that appealed to him. That's how he preferred handling problem situations. He'd always lived by a personal motto of "When in doubt, get out there and stir things up."

Which meant it was time to start stirring.

He narrowed his eyes. Why couldn't he go over to Ms. Jordan Roberts, look her straight in that lovely smoky-eyed face and say, "Lady, sell me your produce market"? He grinned. That would ruffle a feather or two. Or three. And anything that could ruffle *her* feathers interested him greatly.

He watched her examine a carton of cantaloupes, bending low to tug open the stapled lid. Firm muscles played beneath her fitted jeans, drawing his gaze. His grin widened. Nice. Very nice. She lifted one of the large textured melons to her face. Closing her eyes, she inhaled deeply, a tiny smile playing about her lips. The woman understood produce, he conceded. The reverence with which she handled the fruit told him that much.

Rainer spoke to the salesman beside him. "She seems to know her way around all right, but she's too young for this business, Marco, too sweet. It makes me suspicious. There's got to be something else lurking behind that angel face. Something with more of a bite to it."

"She's got a bite, all right," the shorter man confirmed. "It's just that—"

"I knew it! Soft as peach fuzz on the surface, but underneath she's—"

"A nice kid."

Rainer chuckled, his gaze once again on Jordan's trim figure. "Right. A nice kid who bites."

"That's not what I meant. She *is* a nice kid, always has been," Marco insisted obstinately. "Ten years she's bought from us. First with that crazy uncle of hers, now alone. She's always seemed bright and cheerful and—"

"She's worked this business that long?" Rainer tilted his head to one side, his scrutiny of the dark-haired woman sharper than before. She'd moved farther down the dock, stooping to examine a box of Jonathan apples. She didn't look a day over twenty-two—twenty-three at the most. He'd have to readjust his thinking a bit.

"You gonna take her down?" Marco asked anxiously. "I'd think snapping up a woman's livelihood would go against the grain."

Rainer frowned, not appreciating the reminder. That eventuality disturbed him, as well. But this was family business and *nothing* stood in the way of that—not even a pretty brunette with a figure that turned every head on the docks.

He decided to answer Marco honestly. "It would bother me more if she owned the store. But she doesn't. Her uncle owns it. She runs it. If I can win her over to my side, the store will be as good as mine." He paused to consider. "I bet I'd be doing her a favor by taking it off their hands. She can't have much of a life, tied to such a time-consuming business."

Marco looked surprised. "I never thought of it that way. Seems a shame. She's always appeared to be such a happy, contented—"

"Biter?" Rainer's admiring gaze drifted back to Jordan.

The salesman scowled. "It's only when she's pushed that you see her scrappy side."

The younger man suppressed a smile at the combative tone in Marco's voice, intrigued by his spirited defense of the woman. "So much the better," he said gently. "I prefer a fair fight."

Marco groaned. "This is not good. No, sir, it ain't. You don't understand, Rainer. The lady has this little bitty stubborn streak. You swiped her bananas and that's bound to make her a tad testy."

Rainer raised an eyebrow. "I didn't swipe them. You sold them to me."

"Not on purpose, I didn't." The older man's face drooped into deep weather-beaten creases. "I didn't hear they were sold till after I'd promised 'em to you. She'll want 'em back. If she kicks up a fuss and Nick Constantine hears of it, the boss'll have to side with her, no question. After all, those bananas did belong to Ms. Roberts first."

Rainer shrugged. "True. Not that it matters. I'll still have accomplished what I set out to do, regardless of the outcome."

"Which is?"

"To see what she's made of. You think she'll fight me for those bananas, don't you?"

"Don't have to think. I know. She'll fight."

Rainer laughed, clapping a hand on Marco's shoulder. "I'm going to enjoy this. There's nothing a Thorsen relishes more than a friendly tussle with a strong determined opponent." He paused, his grin wicked. "Nothing, that is, except winning."

Marco shifted uneasily. "Listen, I've been thinking. Your father and me, we go way back. Working for Alaric like I used to, I'd do anything for him. Anything. But maybe you could figure out some other way to test Ms. Roberts. She's a nice girl, Rainer. Why would you want to start trouble with her?"

"Because I live for trouble," he said, tongue planted firmly in cheek.

Marco gave an emphatic shake of his head. "Not with her, you don't."

Rainer lifted an eyebrow. "Are we talking deceptive packaging here—as in volcanic possibilities?"

The salesman stirred uncomfortably. "Like I said, only when pushed. Then she's Mount Saint Helens in action. I've seen them both go off." He shuddered. "Don't want to see either do it again."

Rainer studied the woman with renewed interest. "Must have been a beautiful sight."

"Beautiful from a nice safe distance," Marco corrected him. "Not so beautiful when you're standing in the path of the explosion."

"That doesn't sound like you." Rainer frowned. "Where's that famous spirit of adventure I've heard so much about?"

"With my fiftieth birthday, that's where. Both of which are a good ten years past." Marco shoved his pencil behind one ear and tucked his order pad into his pocket. "In all the years she's come down here to buy produce, she's always kept herself to herself. So why do you have to pick on her? Why can't you go after someone else—some*place* else?"

Rainer continued to study Jordan. She stood by a carton of grapes, sampling them before giving a nod of approval. He liked the look of her, the suppleness of her movements. Trim, sleek and graceful—what wasn't to admire? Under normal circumstances he'd be tempted to warm himself in the fire Marco mentioned. But business came first, pleasure...dead second.

"If there was any other way, believe me, I'd take it. Unfortunately that miniature volcano stands between me and something I want. Something I want very much. And once I get her figured out, I'm going to ease her over to one side and take it."

"Yeah?" Marco chuckled. "You'd have better luck easing aside a pallet full of spuds without a forklift. But it might be interesting to see you try."

"Then stand back and get an eyeful." Rainer rubbed his hands briskly. "Just make sure Ms. Roberts knows who has her bananas. I'll be curious to see how she reacts."

"I already told you how she'll react." Marco made the sound of a bomb exploding. "Thar she blows!"

HE WAS STARING at her again; Jordan could feel it. The prickles of reaction started, creating an uncomfortable itch square between her shoulder blades. All morning long he'd watched her and all morning long she'd pretended not to notice.

Until now.

Now she planned to do something about him. She slid her handcart beneath the heavy cardboard boxes of apples on the dock. Angling the stack backward, her arms took the weight of the unwieldy load with ease. She gave the cart an experienced shove and pushed the load over the metal ramp and onto her twelve-foot flatbed, depositing the apples close to the truck's bright green cab.

Her watcher had the advantage of knowing her identity, or at least where she worked. Both her truck doors read Cornucopia Produce Market, the words emblazoned in letters as rosy as the apples she'd just purchased. Now, if she could only figure out *his* identity. So far she'd been unable to catch a glimpse of him. But one way or another, she'd change that.

She swiveled and tossed her long dark braid over her shoulder, leaning her arms across the handles of the upright cart. Casually she scanned the groups of men standing on the cluttered loading dock.

Squinting against the early July sunshine, her gaze instantly zeroed in on him. "Lord help me!" she muttered beneath her breath. If he'd carried a giant hammer in one hand and had lightning bolts flashing from his eyes, she couldn't have been more surprised—or dismayed. *A Viking!* The man staring with such unswerving intensity was a living breathing Viking. She froze, unable to look away.

He was around thirty, tall and broad-shouldered, with an impressive physique. The sun glinted in the bright white-blond of his hair, which he wore short in the front and long in the back, the wavy strands curling over the plaid flannel collar of his shirt. He stood unmoving, openly studying her, his legs spread wide and his arms folded across his large chest. But his immobility didn't fool her. At any moment she expected him to let out a thunderous war cry and come charging her way.

Jordan shivered. She didn't like the sensations he stirred in her. She felt as if someone had hit an internal panic button, and it took every ounce of her self-control to keep the rush of apprehension from showing.

How could she have overlooked this man for most of the morning? It unnerved her to think she'd been so aware of him, while he'd proved so elusive to spot. More importantly though, why had he singled her out? What did he want?

She forced herself to look away, debating how to handle the situation—if there really was anything *to* handle. Perhaps she should find out his identity before she took action. With a decisive shove, she pushed the cart off the truck and toward the salesman writing up her order.

"Who's the Viking, Terry?" she asked quietly.

The salesman didn't even bother looking up. "What Viking?"

She frowned. "The big blond guy. The one who looks like he just stepped out of some Norse legend."

"Oh, yeah. Right. That guy." Terry cleared his throat. "Been wondering the same thing myself. I think he's some high roller Marco brought by to meet the boss."

"Well, your high roller's been staring at me," she informed Terry abruptly.

The salesman chuckled, relaxing. "Yeah, him and every other man on the docks. Face it. You're surrounded by a hoard of lusting animals—also known as men. So what's one more? You should be used to the looks by now."

Jordan rested a foot on a cumbersome carton of lettuce and bit her lip thoughtfully. "It's not that kind of staring. He wants something."

"Tell him to get in line. He's got a long wait." Terry paused in his scribbling and yanked a list from his back pocket, running a gloved finger down it. He stabbed his pencil toward the flats of mushrooms she'd selected. "Those kabobs've gone up another buck, Roberts. Forgot to mention it."

Jordan pushed her unease to one side and concentrated on the job at hand. If the prickles on the back of her neck were anything to go by, the newcomer hadn't budged an inch. She had plenty of time to sort him out once she'd taken care of business.

"Since you forgot to mention the cost went up, you'll have to sell them to me at the old price," Jordan insisted, bartering in the expected manner. "They're not worth a dollar more. Look at the poor things." She selected a mushroom, upending it so he could see where the stem joined the cap. "They've already started to open. And the color—you call this white?"

"Okay. Okay. Ten bucks." He shook his head in disgust. "Boss will fire me for sure over this one."

Jordan smiled at his typical response. "Right. Sure he will. When pigs fly." Nick Constantine would never fire Terry, not when he was the best salesman and haggler on the docks.

She swiftly scanned the long line of stacked boxes left to be loaded, comparing it to the receipt. Oranges vied with kiwifruit, cucumbers with green peppers, the staggering number of fresh sharp odors a source of unending delight.

She checked the order again, her smile fading to a frown. "Wait a minute, Terry. I don't see the bananas. What's happened to them?"

"What bananas?"

She shot him a sharp look. "Don't hand me that. The super deal on the overripes. You were all over me about them when I first walked in."

"Oh. Those bananas."

"Yeah. *Those* bananas."

He yanked the brim of his cap down low over his eyes, ruddy color creeping up his jawline. "You see, they...ah...sort of got sold."

"Sort of got sold?" she snapped. "Sort of—"

Jordan bit off the rest of her sentence, checking her anger. Ranting and raving wouldn't help her case. It was difficult enough working in a male-dominated business without getting a reputation as a shrew. And she'd worked too long and hard to risk losing ground now. Fast thinking and finding the right angle had won many a battle for her—as they would today.

Jordan spoke again, her voice low and even. "The bananas were sold? As in, sold out from under me? I arrived at five-thirty, Terry, which gave me first refusal. You'll remember I didn't do any refusing."

"I remember," Terry agreed, looking everywhere but at her. "How about if next time I—"

She shook her head, not allowing him to finish his offer. "Not next time, Terry. Distress sales are jam on bread in this business. You know that. That's why I come so early. How am I supposed to make a decent living if I can't get my hands on the deals? The competition's death out there."

"Maybe I could squeeze you out a box or two."

"I'm sorry, Terry. A box or two won't do, and I can't afford to shrug this one off." She couldn't afford to shrug any of them off. Not if she was to get her fair share of the bargains.

Terry nodded miserably. "Yeah, I know." He kicked aside the small pile of rotting orange peels and discarded lettuce leaves strewn at his feet. "Give me a few minutes. I—I'll get them back for you."

In all the years she'd dealt with him, she'd never seen Terry so nervous. There shouldn't be such difficulty in sorting out a simple misunderstanding. Jordan frowned.

She'd obviously missed something and she had a pretty good idea what—or who—that something might be.

"Who has my bananas?" she asked.

Terry gave a slight shrug. "Does it matter? I said I'd get them for you."

"*Who?*" she repeated.

The salesman glanced quickly over her shoulder, speaking in a low rushed voice. "You don't want to start anything, Jordan. Not with that particular customer. You'd be better off just letting it go."

"*He* has them?"

Terry nodded. "Every last one. Why don't I speak to Marco? I'm sure he'll straighten everything out."

Jordan thought quickly, then shook her head. "No. Don't bother. I told you our... friend was after something. And I very much doubt it's a pallet load of bananas. This is as good a time as any to find out what he really wants."

"You think he did it so he could meet you?" Terry brightened, the idea clearly appealing to him. "Now why didn't I think of that? Imagine, stealing your bananas just to get your attention. You've got to admit it's a novel approach."

"Yes, imagine resorting to theft," Jordan mocked dryly, "when all he had to do was walk over and introduce himself."

Despite Terry's romantic view of the incident, Jordan suspected the lifting of her bananas had nothing whatsoever to do with romance, or even bananas. The man wanted to instigate a meeting and this was his clever way of going about it. It also forced her to approach him—giving him the advantage. Shrewd, very shrewd.

Jordan appraised the situation. As far as she could tell, she had two choices. She could stand up to him and demand the return of her bananas, or she could shrug it off and walk away. She struggled with her conscience, resisting the part of her urging a hasty retreat. Why for once couldn't she simply turn tail and run? Dogs did it all the time. She liked dogs. They were insightful intelligent creatures.

Of course a dog didn't have the responsibility of a business. If she didn't keep Cornucopia a successful money-making operation, no one else would. And no doubt if Terry's high roller didn't succeed in forcing a confrontation this time, he'd dream up another scheme tomorrow. Better to find out what he wanted now and get it over with.

If only she didn't have this overwhelming urge to roll over and play dead.

She handed Terry his receipt book. "Write up the bananas. I'll be back in a minute. Probably headless, but I'll be back—and *with* the bananas."

The distance she had to traverse never looked so long. But no matter how appealing the idea of doing nothing was, she couldn't stand around all day like a coward. She gazed at her adversary, refusing to be intimidated. It was now or never. Taking a deep breath, Jordan strode determinedly across the cement loading dock. Perhaps it was just her imagination, but it seemed as though every last man jack at the market stopped working to watch.

Stay calm, she warned herself. *Maybe there's a logical explanation for what the banana snatcher has done.*

Or maybe he was just a modern-day Viking. Plunder and pillage could be in his blood.

She skirted a pile of ice chips, a container of green onions and an unhappy-looking Marco. She stopped directly in front of the stranger.

He dwarfed her with his impressive size. Not that his height bothered her. Working on the docks for so long, she'd learned to handle the occasional disparity her five foot five caused. It was the rest of him that proved so disturbing.

His chiseled face, tanned a deep golden brown, sported a squared-off jawline, a determined chin creased by a slight cleft and high prominent cheekbones. Thick blond brows, several shades darker than his hair, set off the vivid green of his deep-set eyes—eyes, she fancifully imagined, filled with the aggressive spirit of his ancestors.

A bright glitter caught her attention and she glanced at his left ear, astonished and intrigued by the tiny gold lightning-bolt earring he wore. The symbol of Thor, she realized with a momentary qualm. A Viking in fact, as well as in appearance.

Her gaze skittered lower. She took in the broad well-muscled shoulders and chest, the lean waist and hips, and finally the thick powerful thighs encased in form-fitting jeans. She swallowed and her gaze flew back to his face. It took every ounce of self-possession to meet those cool mocking eyes with anything approaching equanimity. She braced herself for a similar visual examination—an examination that never came.

Instead he fingered the bridge of his nose, which had obviously been broken at some point in his life—undoubtedly in a brawl—and grinned knowingly. "I see you got my message and decided to come over," he murmured. "Very wise."

Jordan balled her hands into fists, suppressing the temptation to add another crook to his nose. "Was that what it was, a message?" She feigned surprise. "I thought it was your peculiar idea of a joke."

"Oh, it's no joke, Ms. Roberts. I'm very serious."

He knew her name. Which meant she was right; he'd deliberately taken her bananas in order to bring about this confrontation. No matter what Terry thought, this man wasn't interested in *her*. At least, not as a woman.

She found herself thoroughly annoyed—at him because his interest was purely a business one, and at herself for even caring. Jordan pulled herself up short. *No need to get a dented ego,* she scolded silently. He was enough of a threat without that sort of complication.

She glanced at Marco, who stood gazing in fascination at a crushed box of tomatoes tossed to one side of the dock. The poor man couldn't have shown his discomfort any clearer if he'd jumped up and down and screamed it for all the world to hear.

"Why don't we dispense with the games and get down to business?" she suggested. "You have my bananas and I'd appreciate their return."

"*My* bananas," he corrected softly, staring down at her.

How could a single glance from those ice-green eyes burn so? she wondered in trepidation. She crossed to the pallet holding her bananas, her back defiantly stiff. Lifting off a cardboard lid, she flicked the thin plastic cover out of the way and, with a quick twist of her wrist, broke off a banana. After peeling the yellow skin she took a bite, then faced him again. *Claim staked,* she announced silently.

"What do you want, Mr...."

"Thorsen. Rainer Thorsen."

Jordan inhaled sharply, choking on the banana. The Thorsen name and reputation were well-known in the Seattle produce community—as well-known as their Vikinglike appearance and Vikinglike ruthlessness. Also well-known were the dozens of markets they owned and operated, each one at least as large and profitable as Cornucopia. She should have guessed his identity sooner. Her gaze strayed back to the lightning-bolt earring he wore. She should have guessed from that telltale symbol alone.

"My banana too strong for you?" he inquired with mock-solicitude at her continued attempt to clear her windpipe.

Jordan lifted her chin. "*My* banana is just fine, thanks."

"Then you must be choking on the Thorsen name. I've found it does tend to intimidate people."

"I'll struggle to keep that from happening," she informed him, surprised by his levity. "As to the bananas—"

"I suppose, since both of us claim ownership, we'll have to split them." He waggled his eyebrows at her, waiting till she caught his pun.

Jordan's lips twitched. Impossible contradictory man! Didn't he realize what a serious issue this was? "That's one solution, though quite unfair. You know and I know they're really mine. Unfortunately splitting them won't do me any good. I need the full pallet. I don't suppose you're willing to acknowledge prior ownership?"

His teasing facade vanished, exposing the merciless businessman lurking beneath. So the lighthearted charmer was just for show, she realized, filing the information away for future reference.

Rainer shook his head emphatically. "No, I'm not willing to acknowledge any ownership but my own."

Jordan lowered her eyes and thought fast. "I suspected as much." She sighed. "I guess we'll have to settle it in the only reasonable way I know."

"Which is?"

"I'll flip you for them."

He looked down at himself, then at her, his expression doubtful. "Won't be easy. I'm a big guy."

It took her a second, but then she broke down and laughed. This time though, she didn't allow herself to be fooled. "A coin, Mr. Thorsen. We'll flip a coin. Heads or tails?"

"Er, Rainer..." Marco began. He was waved silent.

"Tails," Rainer said and reached into his pocket.

Jordan forestalled him. "Please. Allow me."

If she'd suspected the buyers and workers along the dock were staring before, she was certain of it now. The shouts and occasional curses that usually rang out over the constant noise of the busy marketplace died down. Men in jeans and flannel shirts who normally bustled around the loading area stood in small knots, their attention on the players. Silence reigned.

Steeling her nerves, Jordan stuck a hand into her right pocket and pulled out a nickel. In a practiced move she flicked it high into the air. All eyes watched as the silver coin spun in the early morning light. It tumbled to earth and landed with a ping. After two bounces the coin lay flat on the cement dock.

"Heads," she announced, not displaying the least bit of surprise at the outcome.

Rainer lifted an eyebrow. "Congratulations. I believe that's the first time I've ever been beaten." He frowned. "In fact, I'm certain it's the first time I've ever been beaten." His frown deepened. "I'm not sure I like it."

Jordan smiled. "Get used to it, Mr. Thorsen. I can be pretty resourceful when I have to be." She leaned down with studied indifference, picked up the coin and pocketed it. Curling her pinkie fingers into her mouth, she gave a high shrill whistle. As though by magic, Terry was at her side.

"Please put my bananas on the truck, Terry," Jordan instructed briskly. She glanced up at Rainer and smiled again. "Nice doing business with you, Mr. Thorsen." She hesitated. "Our business *is* completed, isn't it?"

He folded his arms across his chest and shook his head, staring at her with narrowed eyes. "Not quite. But it'll keep, Ms. Roberts. It'll keep." He held out a large callused hand. "Until next time."

Faltering, but only for a moment she slipped her hand into his. The man's handshake was as strong and firm as he was. He tightened his grip, refusing to release her. Her gaze flashed to his and she nearly flinched. She couldn't mistake the fierce determination in his expression.

"I'm accustomed to getting what I want, Ms. Roberts. You'd do well to remember that."

Not trusting her voice, she nodded. Carefully, she tugged her hand away and headed back across the loading dock. The distance seemed even longer than before and she was conscious of every eye on her. She touched the double-headed coin in her right pocket. How long would it take for Thorsen to learn how she'd tricked him?

She reached her end of the dock and Terry scurried up to her. "You know who that is?" he demanded in a nervous whisper.

"Yeah, I know."

"And still you pulled that little stunt with one of your double-sided coins?"

She turned on him. "They were *my* bananas. I told you I'd get them back one way or the other. Unfortunately it had to be the other." She glanced at the salesman, not hiding her concern. "Do you think Marco will tell him what I did?"

Terry shook his head. "Not likely. He used to work for the Thorsens a few years back, so he still has a certain loyalty to them. But he's crazy about you. We all are. If anyone tells Thorsen, it'll be Mr. Constantine. Once he gets wind of it he'll spill the beans, if only because he thinks it's such a huge joke."

"Nuts."

"You got that right." Terry leaned toward her, lowering his voice. "I'd hoped to avoid a confrontation with him, get you to forget about those bananas. But it's too late for that. You'd better know, Jordan—the Thorsens have always bought their produce from houses closer to Boeing Field. I hear Marco convinced them to give us a try. You realize what that means, don't you?"

"Another showdown tomorrow?"

"That, and more." Terry's expression was unusually serious. "Thorsen buys big, real big, and he always, *always* gets what he wants. If he decides to buy from Constantine, he'll keep two of our salesmen hustling and more importantly, he'll pay same as everyone but you—cash on the barrel head. None of this line-of-credit stuff the boss has been willing to give Cornucopia. And that's a lot of bucks."

"Nick must be jumping through hoops," she muttered.

"He ain't crying in his beer, that's for sure. Mr. Constantine may think your little stunt funny now. But if he loses any business because of it, you'll find yourself out on your pretty little keister—no matter how close you are to the boss's daughter."

"That's not fair!" she protested. "Andrea and I have always kept our friendship separate from the business. Cornucopia has a line of credit because we're a safe risk, not because of personalities."

But her concern deepened. She didn't like the sound of this. Nick Constantine was a hardheaded businessman. If Thorsen decided to make things uncomfortable for her, Nick might choose to go with the money—and to hell with ten years' worth of loyalty.

Her mouth firmed. She wasn't beaten yet. In fact, she hadn't even begun to fight. "I may not be in the same league as the Thorsens, but Cornucopia is nothing to sneeze at."

Terry sighed, shaking his head. "It is compared to the Thorsens. If it meant getting their business, the old man would sell his own daughter. Hell, he'd *give* her away. So, don't say I didn't warn you."

Jordan stirred uneasily. "I'll consider myself duly warned."

She glanced over her shoulder and down the long length of the dock. The Viking was still there, standing and staring once again, his brawny arms folded across his chest. As clearly as if he'd shouted the words at her, she knew their business—whatever that might be—was far from completed.

RAINER WATCHED JORDAN climb into the cab of her truck and start the engine. He'd been impressed by her. Very impressed. He hadn't seen any volcanic activity during their confrontation, but that didn't bother him. Once she found out what he really wanted, he bet he'd see a major eruption.

A damned shame, really. Jordan Roberts fascinated him. He sensed a shrewdness behind those cool direct eyes—eyes an intriguing shade between blue and gray. He'd discovered that her face held more than beauty; it contained a wealth of character. The rounded chin and dark angled eyebrows suggested determination. The high cheekbones and firm set of lips and jaw hinted at an inner strength lacking in most women he knew. Even the way she'd subdued that mane of curly black hair warned of her need for control.

He rubbed the bridge of his nose thoughtfully. Black velvet over steel. An intriguing image. It was both enlightening—and revealing. Probably more revealing than she'd have liked.

"Judging from her reaction over those bananas," he said, turning to Marco, "there's little doubt how she'll respond once she learns I'm after Cornucopia. I have to admit she's got nerve. That was quite a gamble she took with the coin toss."

"If you say so," Marco muttered, mopping his brow.

Rainer frowned at the salesman. "I say so." He tilted his head to one side, analyzing his options. "Looks like I have three choices. I can either buy Cornucopia out, go around it or break its hold on the north end with a competing market." He grinned. "And since I've never been one to go around an obstacle when I can bust right through it, I guess we can eliminate at least one of those choices."

Marco shifted uneasily. "I don't know. Sometimes it's faster to skirt a mountain. Tunneling through can take time."

Rainer was unswayed. "Tunnels make for a shorter trip over the long haul. Besides, it's cleaner. Cornucopia is going down, one way or another. It's best not to prolong the agony." That resolved, he gave a decisive nod. "Well, Ms. Roberts. You have your bananas. But soon, I'll have you."

CHAPTER TWO

LATER THAT MORNING, Jordan walked through the front door of Cornucopia Produce Market—and into the one place that was more home to her than any spot on earth.

Another hour remained before the doors opened for business. She looked around, releasing a happy contented sigh. It gave her a good feeling, being here in the very store her grandfather had started, continuing the family tradition.

She crossed the floor to stand in front of a wall of photos—ones that traced the history of the market from its inception to the present day. She took pride in this history. It gave her a connection, a sense of belonging—something she and her Uncle Cletus both appreciated.

It also represented her heritage, one she struggled on a daily basis to preserve. She wanted to do her parents and grandparents proud, to have their spirit live on through her efforts—and through Cornucopia.

Sometimes, though, she felt woefully inadequate and it worried her. Ever since Uncle Cletus's stroke a year ago, more and more of the responsibility for the store fell on her shoulders; the thought of losing her last remaining relative was a nagging concern. *Buck up,* she ordered. *You're letting Thorsen get to you. It's your job—you can handle it. Just like your father and your uncle and your grandfather before you.*

Grandpa Joe had been the store's first proprietor. With his passing nearly twenty years ago, her father, Jake, and his brother, Cletus, had run things. Now that her uncle was all the family she had left and since she had his physical well-being to consider, Jordan had taken charge. Someday she'd own Cornucopia outright.

A smile teased the corners of her mouth. At least she'd own the store once it brought in enough to pay for Uncle Cletus's retirement. In the meantime, work awaited.

She'd left the truck parked by the side door, two employees busy unloading it. At a guess, Uncle Cletus and his friend and co-worker, Walker, were in the far back, preoccupied with their never-ending checker game. She glanced at her watch. Five minutes remained—ten if she was lucky—before mass confusion broke out. And she intended to take full advantage of those few minutes of rare peace and quiet. She wanted to savor every second of this brief stolen time alone in her store.

Strolling up and down the bright sunlit aisles, she checked each display. Some counters were swept clean, waiting to be loaded to groaning capacity with fruit and crisp fresh vegetables. Others were already filled with less perishable items, attractively arranged and ready for purchase by the early shoppers who gathered at the front door on the dot of nine.

Progressing aisle by aisle, she sorted through the apples and dried beans, squash and potatoes that covered the huge gingham-skirted counters. Her father had built these counters, and she noted with pride their peaked design, like the roof of a house, rather than a conventional flat tabletop.

She ran an eagle eye over everything. Nothing escaped her—not the bit of dust collecting in a back corner, nor the early signs of wear on the edges of the green-checked table skirt, nor the lopsided sign stuck in the middle of a pile of

Yellow Finn potatoes. She took note of each imperfection. Before the end of the day she'd see every last one corrected.

Jordan nodded, satisfied. High-quality produce and reasonable prices—that, in large part, was what made Cornucopia so popular. But the real secret to their success was the warm traditional "feeling of family" that characterized the market and made it that extra bit special. Yes, *family*. She knew all about the importance of family.

"Uncle Cletus," she called, heading for the back of the store. "Wait till you see what I bought today."

"Not now, Jordan," her uncle responded. A man in his early sixties swept aside the heavy canvas curtain separating the main store from the employee lounge. In one hand he held an avocado, in the other a sugar beet. "Three more jumps and I'll have Walker trounced."

"Six," came the obdurate retort. "Put back my man."

With great reluctance, Cletus returned the sugar beet to a large painted checkerboard that covered the surface of the packing crate set between them. "Don't know why you have to be so picky about a bunch of silly rules," he muttered. "You know that piece will be mine in two more moves."

"Three."

Jordan struggled to keep from smiling. Uncle Cletus might misunderstand if he saw her grin, and she wouldn't hurt him for anything. Besides, it wasn't amusement she felt in his ongoing contest with Walker, as much as fond affection. "It's time to set up, Uncle Cletus," she announced.

"In a minute, my dear."

She leaned down and planted a kiss on the top of his balding head. "Go ahead and finish. But I should warn you that I just ran across the dullest eggplant you ever saw."

Cletus looked up in alarm. "Dull?"

"Plump, firm and the darkest purple you could want. But dull as a tarnished penny," she informed him. "Don't you worry about it, though. I wouldn't dream of interrupting your checker game.''

"You can't put out dull eggplant," Cletus said in censorious tones. "What would our customers think? If the eggplant isn't just right, the customers won't buy it."

"No, they won't," Jordan concurred.

He frowned. "If the customers don't buy, the cash registers stop ringing."

"True," she acknowledged, waiting.

"And if the cash registers stop ringing—" His eyes widened in alarm and without another word, he swept the sugar beets and avocados off the crate and into a box. "You lose, Walker. Time to get to work. Come along now, we have eggplant to tend."

Jordan permitted herself a small smile of satisfaction. Diligence wasn't her uncle's strong point, so she felt completely justified in using the one weapon guaranteed to work—basic human greed. Such an endearing flaw in an otherwise warm and loving personality. Oh, well. All was fair in love, war and turnip-touting—because as far as she was concerned, this business was one constant battle.

"Hey, you forgot to take the avocados and sugar beets with you," she said, watching in exasperation as the two men hurried off without the box of produce.

Family. You can't work with 'em, and you can't work without 'em. She shook her head and grinned, carrying the box of ''checker'' vegetables into the store and leaving Cletus and Walker to organize and set up the displays. Arranging the produce as attractively as possible was their area of expertise. Her uncle seemed to have a knack for combining colors and textures, a knack that contributed greatly to increased sales.

Jordan headed for the employee lunchroom, where she grabbed a yogurt from the refrigerator and sat down. She pulled her receipts from her pocket and, calculator at her elbow, began to figure out the costs, circling items that would need price changes.

It was a routine she followed religiously, just as all her workers had their set routines. One pair of employees unloaded the truck and carted the various boxes directly into the store or into the huge walk-in cooler at the back of the shop. Cletus and Walker took care of setting up while she did the paperwork and made new display signs. At precisely 9 a.m., her workers manned the cash registers and the store opened. She smiled. At least it should operate that way. The reality was often different.

It didn't take her long to do the pricing. She spooned up the last of the yogurt, then swiftly made a list of the sign changes. Finished, she slipped her bibbed apron off its hook and put it on over her T-shirt and jeans. Now for the signs. Fancy billboard placards blanketed the outside of the market, and each day she used colored markers to create new ads to tack over the old, promoting the day's specials. Within twenty minutes, nine bright signs were drafted, carted outside and stapled into place.

She reentered the store to find the mass confusion she'd anticipated reigning freely. Two employees, standing amidst stacks of banana boxes, were engaged in a heated dispute about where to display the fruit. A third employee stood idly by filing her fingernails. Jordan glanced over at Uncle Cletus and shook her head. He clutched a shiny eggplant to his chest and glared at Walker. Walker, a mulish expression on his face, glared right back.

Okay. Everything status quo. Which meant it was time to get the show on the road, starting with the bananas.

"Leroy, Andy, the bananas should be in front. Put up as many as possible. We need them out before they start spotting or we'll be eating banana bread till Christmas." She caught Michelle's eye. "I don't want to ruin your nail job, but how about getting the empty boxes to the trash Dumpster and the cooler organized."

Satisfied by the instant response to her instructions, she turned her attention to Uncle Cletus and his monosyllabic companion. With a determined stride, she headed for the back of the store.

"You have to move those radishes," she could hear Cletus order Walker. "You know they're politically incompatible with my eggplant."

"Aren't," Walker retorted with stubborn persistence.

Cletus drew himself up, his voice rising. "Radishes belong with green onions and celery and the rest of the Democrats. Eggplants are Republican down to their toenails and never the twain shall meet."

"Don't have toenails."

"Don't argue!"

Jordan stepped between them, her hands on her hips. "Uncle Cletus, Walker. I thought we had an agreement about this sort of thing." The two men stared at the floor, abashed. "No politics in the store, remember?"

"Normally I wouldn't dream of it," Uncle Cletus claimed self-righteously. He spared a scowl for Walker. "But in this case, there's no getting around it. Fact is fact, right is right, and eggplant is Republican."

"Uncle Cletus . . ."

He smiled benignly and put an arm around her shoulders, drawing her off to one side. "Listen my dear, you've done very well these past few years. Very well, indeed. But you still have one or two things left to learn before the store is yours and I retire to my chicken ranch in New Mexico."

Jordan sighed. "Arizona, Uncle Cletus. You want to retire to Arizona."

"Exactly. But I can't do that until I'm positive you comprehend the political and philosophical mind-set of produce."

"I wasn't aware that food had a mind-set," she murmured.

He offered her a pitying look. "I'm not surprised. It takes a keen eye to spot it." He patted her shoulder. "Which is why I'm here to help. Take eggplant, for example. Hates radishes. Downright despises them. You can't even put the two on the same counter. Disastrous results if you do."

Jordan snuck a quick peek at her watch. "Uncle Cletus, I know this is important, but—"

"Vital. Absolutely vital. Put your eggplant with rutabagas and turnips and it's an entirely different story. They get on like ants and a picnic." He paused, his expression reflective. "You might get away with mixing eggplants with peppers on the odd occasion." He fixed her with a stern gaze. "But never red peppers. Green bells only."

"I'll remember that, Uncle Cletus. Now if we could—"

"Which brings us back to the issue of radishes."

Jordan closed her eyes. "The radishes?"

"It's not a matter to be trifled with. The radishes cannot be put anywhere near the eggplant."

She nodded decisively. "When you're right, you're right. The political ramifications would be devastating." She turned and faced her uncle's helper. "Walker, the radishes go. Put them by the..." She glanced at Cletus, her eyebrows raised.

He gave it a moment's careful deliberation. "The green onions and celery. That should allow them all to ponder the prevailing economic climate."

"See to it," she ordered briskly, then announced to the room at large, "Five minutes until we open. Let's get the aisles cleared. Leroy, get this water mopped or we'll be up to our asparaguses in lawsuits. Michelle, you're on cash register one. Andy, get those potatoes sorted. Let's go, people! We're running late.''

But then, they were always running late. Just once she'd like to have the market picture-perfect when she opened the front doors to the first customer. Confusion and disarray bothered her—a lot. Unfortunately in this business they were a fact of life, one she'd learned to live with.

She hurried to the front of the store and stopped short, a small groan escaping her. Mrs. Swenson headed the line of customers. Jordan wasn't surprised. She'd started the day with a Viking; naturally she'd continue it with the Norse answer to Attila the Hun. Heaven help the tomatoes, because dear Mrs. Swenson had a grip that could squeeze blood from a hazelnut.

Jordan unlocked the doors and smiled a greeting. Within seconds the store filled with shoppers. As she'd predicted, Mrs. Swenson marched straight for the tomatoes. At the last minute she veered toward the eggplant. Jordan, knowing trouble when she saw it, followed her. Combining Mrs. Swenson with her grip of iron and Uncle Cletus with his precious eggplant could only mean a combustion of the most elemental kind.

Sure enough, Uncle Cletus took a defensive stance in front of his display, his arms spread wide. Not that that deterred Mrs. Swenson. The stocky woman brushed him aside with no more effort than it would take to swat a pesky fly.

"Your eggplant looks tired," she announced, picking one up and inspecting it with meticulous care.

"Tired?" Uncle Cletus's voice held a strangled quality. He snatched the eggplant from her and cradled it protectively in his arms. "My dear woman, I'll have you know these eggplants are in their prime of life."

Mrs. Swenson sniffed. "What would you know about an eggplant's prime, when you don't even know your own? Men think their prime starts when they crawl out of their diapers and ends with the last nail in their coffin."

"You mean it doesn't?" Uncle Cletus grumbled.

The look she shot him could have shriveled watermelons. She picked up another eggplant and shook it at him. "A week ago these were in their prime. Today they're just plain tired." She dropped the mangled vegetable back onto the pile. "There's nothing more pathetic than tired eggplant."

"Why, Mrs. Swenson, how nice to see you this morning," Jordan interrupted. "Have you seen our wonderful deal on bananas?"

"Good morning, Jordan. Yes, I've seen it. But you know I only buy top-quality produce. Those aren't even fit for banana bread." She reached for a third eggplant, but was forestalled when another voice intruded on their conversation—a deep familiar voice, one that caused Jordan to stiffen in alarm.

"Try this one, Mrs. Swenson," Rainer Thorsen suggested. He cut neatly between them and plucked a large eggplant from the back of the display. He cupped it in his hands and held it up so the overhead lights gleamed off the rich purple skin. Then he lifted it to his face and inhaled deeply. "Yes, this is the perfect one."

The Norwegian woman eyed him with equal parts curiosity and suspicion. "Do you think so?"

"Yes. Definitely." He took her work-worn hand in his, placing it around the vegetable with care. "Be gentle now. Eggplant is like a beautiful woman. Squeeze too hard and you'll bruise her. And that would be a sin, don't you think?"

"Not another one," Jordan muttered rudely, rolling her eyes. "First politics, now sex. I swear these vegetables see more action than I do."

"I—oh—oh yes..." Mrs. Swenson said in apparent fascination.

"Even the shape is womanly," Rainer continued, "round and full-bodied, the skin, warm and firm and smooth." He grasped her other hand so they held the eggplant between them. "Do you feel that—how it invites the touch? Eggplant is one of the most sensuous vegetables you'll find."

Jordan listened in amazement as Mrs. Swenson gave a deep heartfelt sigh. Eggplant, sensuous? But apparently the woman agreed with him, because she nodded, her faded blond topknot bobbing up and down.

"Sensuous. Very sensuous," she repeated breathlessly.

Rainer eased the eggplant into the plastic basket she carried on her arm. "Not as sensuous as tomatoes, of course." He slipped his hand beneath her elbow and, sparing a quick glance at Jordan, said, "Coming?" before leading her customer toward the tomatoes. "You can't buy your man eggplant, *Kjæreste,* and not tempt him with love's most infamous vegetable."

"Sweetheart." Mrs. Swenson sighed again. "My husband used to call me that."

"Feed him more tomatoes," Rainer responded promptly, "and he will again."

"Well I'll be a pickled herring," Jordan muttered, staring after them. She didn't know whether to be grateful, annoyed or suspicious. Suspicion won out. Who did he think he was, Svengali? And what had he done to *her* customer? At a guess, charmed Mrs. Swenson into buying more produce in one day than she had in the past month.

Jordan drummed her fingers against the wooden counter, her eyes narrowed. That golden-haired smooth-talking devil incarnate wanted something. And if she was wise, she'd find out what. Pronto.

Before she could act, Uncle Cletus tapped her on the shoulder and gestured toward Rainer. "Who is that?" he asked, intrigued.

"Trouble, with a capital T."

Her uncle shook his head. "Impossible. A man with such an instinctive understanding of the basic nature of eggplant can't be all that bad."

"Trust me on this," she said dryly. "'Bad' doesn't begin to describe the man."

Determined to find out why he'd come, she headed after Rainer. She didn't buy two coincidences in a row, especially when the first wasn't one. So, what did he want? Not the bananas; that didn't make sense. Or did it? She paused in midstride, her right hand straying to her pocket. Maybe he'd found out about the coin trick and had come to reclaim what he deemed his property. Jordan smiled coolly. If so, she'd soon disabuse him of the notion.

By the time she caught up with Rainer and Mrs. Swenson, they were examining the tomatoes. Her gaze snagged on Rainer's lean fingers stroking a plump red tomato. He was right, she thought. Tomatoes *were* sensuous. Certainly the way he touched them was. And suddenly she knew she'd never be able to think about them the same way again.

She swallowed.

The man had an exquisite touch—what a shame to waste it on an inanimate vegetable. Not, she hastened to assure herself, that she'd care to experience his caresses personally. But to give such loving attention to a tomato?

He bent down and whispered something in Mrs. Swenson's ear. To Jordan's astonishment, the woman turned as red as the vegetable he held and let out a snort of laughter.

"It's the truth," he insisted. "If you don't believe me, ask Jordan."

"Ask me what?" she said, not certain she wanted to know.

Rainer held up the tomato, turning it. "That one of the names for this vegetable is the 'love apple.'"

As much as it went against the grain, she forced herself to agree with him. "That was one name for them, among others."

"Quite right. Also the wolf peach—"

"The mad apple—"

"And the rage apple." He offered the tomato to Mrs. Swenson. "But to me, it will always be . . . the love apple."

So he liked to play games, did he? Well, she played games and quite ably, too. "Tomatoes," Jordan stated with determination. "Low in calories, high in nutrition. They contain vitamins A, B1, B2 and C—"

"Once considered poisonous," he broke in, shooting her a wicked look, "they were later considered poisonous only to the chaste. And long believed an aphrodisiac, they were avoided by all proper maidens who guarded their virtue." He selected another tomato and offered it to Jordan, along with a mocking grin. "Shall I tempt your virtue?"

She took the proffered fruit. "*Lycopersicon esculentum,* literally 'juicy wolf peach.' A member of the nightshade family, the fruit is the only edible portion. In actuality a berry, it is legally a vegetable."

Rainer stepped closer, his green eyes gleaming with amusement. "There are literally thousands of varieties, such as the Bonny Best, the Atom, the Droplet—"

"The Cannibal, the Jetfire, the Dutchman—"

He interrupted, his voice low and intimate. "The Moon Glow, the Perfecta, the Terrific . . ." He paused, his gaze unbearably seductive, and suddenly Mrs. Swenson ceased to exist. "The Crimson Cushion, the White Beauty, the Red Glow." His voice lowered still further, caressing every syllable. "And the Venus."

She spoke crisply. It was a struggle, but she did it, emphasizing each chilly word. "The Subarctic, the Snowball, the Toy Boy, the Crackproof—"

"You forgot the Superman."

She raised her chin and stared him straight in the eye. "And the When-Hell-Freezes-Over."

A delighted grin crossed Rainer's face. "I must have missed that one. I'll have to get out my Burpee catalogue and look it up."

"Well, which kind of tomatoes are these?" Mrs. Swenson wanted to know, peering from one to the other in bewilderment.

Jordan didn't miss a beat. "They're the When-H—"

"Behave-yer-selves," he inserted smoothly, quelling her with a glance. "Behave-yer-selves Beefstakes."

"That's . . . different," Mrs. Swenson said. "Where do they come up with such peculiar names?"

"From peculiar people with strange senses of humor," Jordan couldn't resist saying.

Rainer inclined his head. "Thank you, my dear, though I prefer eccentric to peculiar."

"We can't have everything we want."

He gave a little sigh. "You weren't listening this morning at the wholesale market, were you?" His relentless gaze intimidated her, made threats she knew he'd keep. "You'll find I always get what I want."

"Not always, Mr. Thorsen," she dared to remind him. "You lost the bananas."

He didn't immediately respond, instead placing half a dozen tomatoes into Mrs. Swenson's basket. Then he said gently, "I only lost if the bananas were my ultimate objective. They weren't." He allowed Jordan to mull that over, before adding, "I get what I go after. Some things take a little time, but in the end, I get them just the same. I always do. I suggest you remember that." He smiled down at Mrs. Swenson. "Shall we move on to the roots?"

I always do. His threat hung in the air. Jordan couldn't have moved if her life depended on it. For the first time she knew fear—honest to goodness, belly-deep, stomach-curdling fear. What did he want? It was imperative she find out. *Think, darn it, think!*

Unfortunately her instinctive ability to grasp a situation chose that moment to desert her. Normally she could size up an individual with no problem, sensing his or her strengths and weaknesses. But this man was all strengths and no weaknesses. And without a weakness, how was she expected to decide on an angle of approach?

Should she force the issue? Should she charm him? Should she toss him out on his lightning-bolt earring? What angle would work best? Well, even without an angle doing something was better than doing nothing at all. She started after him.

"Jordan?"

Michelle caught her a few feet short of her goal. Rainer glanced over at them and, as though aware of her frustration at the interruption, winked.

She dragged her attention from Rainer to the petite blond standing at her elbow. "Yes, what is it?"

"That student you talk to all the time, Seth what's-his-name, is here. He wants to run a tab on his order again."

"Do it."

The younger girl hesitated. "Uh, you see, his purchases are sort of high this time—twenty dollars and fifty-four cents—and that tab of his hasn't gotten any smaller."

Jordan chuckled. "Sure it has. It's easy. Just take the old tab, wad it up in a little ball and stick it in that round metal barrel beneath the register."

"The trash can?" Michelle's voice squeaked in disbelief.

"You got it. Then get out a new piece of paper and write twenty fifty-four on it. Voilà. Small tab again."

"But..."

Jordan smiled gently. "Honey, Seth's struggling to work his way through school. Look at this as our contribution to higher education."

"You mean our contribution to a smooth-talking con artist," Michelle muttered.

Jordan lifted an eyebrow, the tiny signal of disapproval enough to silence the girl. "Don't be so suspicious. Try thinking of him like you do the electric company. You pay the bill and end up with a brighter day."

"Yeah, well you must have a lot of bright days, since Seth isn't the only customer whose tab gets filed away under the register." She held up her hands in surrender. "But you're the boss. I hear and obey."

"Smart move." Jordan glanced toward Michelle's register. "And be nice to Seth. He's looking a little worried over there."

"Yeah, I can guess why."

"Michelle," Jordan warned, "I mean it. He has a lot of pride. Don't dent it."

That said, she looked at Rainer. To her surprise a frown creased his face and she realized he'd overheard her conversation with Michelle—and disapproved. She couldn't hide her indignation. Really! It was her store. It was her produce. And it was her customer. The one thing it wasn't, was any of his business.

Before she could say as much, he returned his attention to Mrs. Swenson. With a friendly smile, he shifted her basket to his arm, leaning close to discuss the merits of sweet potatoes. As though unable to resist, he reached out and rearranged the display in front of him.

Uncle Cletus approached her next. "What's that fellow doing?" he muttered in her ear.

"He's—"

"I'll tell you what he's doing. He's touching my produce. He's changing things around. Look, look! He moved that yam. I *wanted* that yam there. That yam wanted to *stay* there. And *he* moved it."

Jordan swallowed a smile. "Perhaps he doesn't understand yams quite as well as eggplant."

Her uncle snorted. "I'm beginning to think he doesn't understand eggplants, either. It was probably just a lucky guess."

"He can't help sorting the produce. It's not meant as an insult. It's . . . it's habit," she said, and realized the truth of her comment. His restless movements—the scanning, shifting and arranging—were as natural to him as to her. As natural to them both as breathing. She could choose to resent his presumptuousness, but there was no point. It came unconsciously, with no offense intended.

"Habit?" Cletus said in a querulous tone. "Is he in produce, too? What's his name?"

"Rainer Thorsen."

Her uncle froze, then used a word she'd never heard him say before. She stared at him, his panicked expression turning her astonishment to concern.

"What is it?" she asked. "What's wrong?"

"What does he want?" he fired at her. "What's he doing here?"

She shook her head. "I don't know." And that was it in a nutshell. Rainer Thorsen. A Viking. A man of action. A conqueror. What had he chosen to conquer this time?

"Get him out!" her uncle demanded. "He's trouble."

"I already told you that. Remember? Trouble with a capital T. But you were sure that a man with..." She groped for an exact quote. "'A man with such an instinctive understanding of the basic nature of eggplant can't be all that bad.'"

"You were right. I was wrong. He *is* trouble. So get rid of him."

"How do you suggest I do that?" she asked, attempting to be reasonable. "Go up to the man and say, this store ain't big enough for the two of us? You and your lightning bolt get outta town?"

"This is no time to joke!"

For some unknown reason, Jordan found herself taking Rainer's side—the man was clearly a bad influence. "What's the worst he can do? Look at him—he's sold more to Mrs. Swenson in one day than we have in a month of Sundays."

"I can survive without Mrs. Swenson's business."

"What about Edie, and Mrs. Lawsen? They've been shopping for over half an hour and they've filled up two baskets each. Why? Because they can't take their eyes off our friend. It's a wonder they haven't tripped over each other's tongues—though I do live in hope."

"That's disgraceful!"

She didn't understand what had gotten into her, but she couldn't resist adding, "Mmm. It's also good for business. Maybe I can hire him to come in once a week and flex his biceps. I could even put up a sign—one basket of produce for fifteen minutes' viewing time."

Uncle Cletus glared at her. "You going to kick that man out or not?" he demanded.

"Not."

"Don't say I didn't warn you." Muttering furiously beneath his breath, he stomped off in a huff.

Jordan felt ashamed of herself. She shouldn't needle Uncle Cletus that way, not when he only had their best interests at heart. She'd apologize to him. Their relationship was too precious to risk. Which meant that she should confront Rainer and find out what he wanted, then see if she couldn't—politely—usher him out the door.

Squaring her shoulders, she joined him at the berry counter. Mrs. Swenson clutched a second basket in her hand, this one overflowing with nectarines, grapes and raspberries. "Thank you, Mr. Thorsen...Rainer." The older woman dimpled at him. "You've been such a help. I can't wait to tell Ivar all about the tomatoes."

"Love apples," he corrected her.

She blushed. "Love apples." And with that, she trotted toward the checkout stand.

Once Mrs. Swenson was out of hearing range, Jordan said, "You two certainly got on like a house on fire. I don't suppose you want a full-time job? You have quite a way with my customers, particularly those of the female persuasion."

"Don't be snide," he admonished. "You should be grateful. I even managed to sell her some bananas."

"How did you pull that off?" she asked, curiosity getting the better of her. "Not more love potions or cute legends, I hope."

He grinned. "No sex, no politics, just plain, old dry-as-dust fact. I told her bananas were like people—they improved with age."

Jordan nodded, secretly impressed. "I like it."

"I'm glad. Because if you continue to give the produce away, you're going to need every extra sale I can drum up."

"Try minding your own business." She smiled sweetly. "It'll save your poor nose another crook."

He didn't look at all intimidated. "So. Come to give me my marching orders, have you?"

She chuckled. "How did you guess?"

"It wasn't difficult." He glanced toward the curtained-off section at the back of the store. "You shouldn't have told your uncle my identity. You scared him."

She wouldn't ask how he knew that Cletus was her uncle, nor how he knew what she and Uncle Cletus had discussed. Clairvoyance, telepathy, omniscience—nothing seemed beyond him. "Does he have reason to be scared?" she asked instead.

He didn't answer, which was answer enough. Darn! Why, every time she got within arm's length of the man, did she forget he meant trouble? She wouldn't forget again. She'd engrave it on her forehead, if necessary, but she wouldn't forget.

Jordan lifted her chin. The game was over. It was time to get serious. She'd thought of exactly three angles of approach, admittedly all less than brilliant, to use in her dealings with him. She could charm him. She could physically eject him. Or she could force him to admit what he wanted.

She'd already tried charm; it hadn't gotten her anywhere. But then, she never was much good at charm. And tossing him out, presuming she could, would only bring a temporary end to their conversation. That narrowed her choices a whole heck of a lot. Like down to one. Somehow, forcing this man into a confession seemed the poorest, and most ludicrous, choice of all.

Maybe she could beg.

"Would you care to tell me what you want—before you leave?" She almost sighed aloud. She never was much good at begging.

He smiled then, his ruthless, Viking I'm-going-to-win-no-matter-what smile. "I don't want much," he said gently. "Just your store."

CHAPTER THREE

RAINER REACHED OUT, his finger nearly brushing her cheek. "Your eyes have gone from blue to gray," he commented conversationally. "Does that mean something?"

Jordan jerked her head back. "Take it as storm warnings and stand clear."

"Really?" He cocked an eyebrow. "It's typhoons I need to watch for, not volcanoes?"

"What the hell does the weather have to do with this discussion?" She reacted like a tigress defending her young. "Are you crazy or something? You come into my store, bother my customers, rearrange our displays, throw out blatant threats and warnings, and then have the unmitigated gall to say you want my store?"

"Your uncle's," he interrupted softly.

"What?"

"Your uncle's store," he repeated.

He took a step closer, following when she backed hastily away. How ridiculous to feel such instinctive fear when people hemmed them in on all sides. Yet she did. Something about his determined gaze and purposeful stride reminded her of a stalking predator. He cornered her against a huge bin of watermelons.

"What are you doing?" she gasped.

"Clarifying a few things. For your information, I did not bother your customers, I showed you the appropriate way to handle a troublemaker."

"Thanks," she muttered. "I'll try romancing Mrs. Swenson next time she comes in, though I doubt I'll get the same results."

He grinned. "I'd worry if you did. Moving right along, if I rearranged any displays, put it down to—" he appeared to debate "—an irresistible compulsion to touch things I like. There's a lot in this store I feel irresistibly compelled to touch." His gaze eased over her meaningfully. "But lucky for you I've limited myself to the produce."

"Congratulations. Have a raspberry."

His look hinted at retribution. "Next point. I never make threats or warnings, blatant or otherwise. I make promises. And I *always* keep my promises."

"Like you *always* get what you want?" she taunted. What had gotten into her? Why couldn't she keep her mouth shut? She must have some fatalistic death wish that caused her to spout words guaranteed to bring a fast end to a short life.

He moved even closer, edging her up against the bin. "I'm so glad we understand each other."

She wiggled away from him in the only direction available—up and onto the watermelons. Not only did she feel ridiculous, she was fairly certain she looked ridiculous, too. The crowning glory would be for him to say as much.

"Comfy?" he inquired in a polite voice.

She gritted her teeth. "Exceedingly."

"Good. Final point. Correct me if I'm wrong—I understand this store belongs to one Cletus Roberts, not a Ms. Jordan Roberts. Are my sources mistaken?"

Alarm flared through her. "How do you know that?"

"Was it a secret?"

She shook her head. "Of course not, but—"

"That means any business discussions I have regarding Cornucopia Produce should be with him, not some overly protective wise-cracking impertinent employee."

Overly protective? Of course she was overly protective! Family tended to make a person that way. Fury took hold. She placed the palms of her hands square on his chest and shoved with all her might. He didn't budge. She stared at him, both surprised and dismayed. Good grief. This man was built like a rock, with the stubborn immobility to match. Well, stone could be chiseled. She might not be Michelangelo, but she'd be delighted to give it her best whack.

"Look, Mr. Thorsen. This store is a *family* business. Any decisions made about this store are *family* decisions. So whether you like the idea or not, you're stuck dealing with me. Those are the facts. Deal with them, or deal yourself out."

"Volcanoes, typhoons and now fire and brimstone. I like it," he murmured.

Jordan glared at him in exasperation. The man's elevator definitely stopped shy of the penthouse. "In the meantime, move your carcass, or you'll be wearing watermelon on that Viking head of yours instead of horns!"

For a minute she thought she'd gone too far. His eyes narrowed, the green as chilly as an arctic sea. Then a small rumbling began deep in his chest, spreading and growing. He tilted his head back and laughed, the sound rich and full and attractive, turning the heads of the shoppers.

"Yes! Now I understand," he said. He caught hold of her chin, tilting it up, his firm grip curbing any resistance. "So, you're a Valkyrie. I should have known."

"What's that?" she demanded suspiciously.

A smile edged the corners of his mouth. "A warrior maiden. In old Norse legend, they swept fallen heroes off to Valhalla. Is that what you want? To carry me off?"

"And dump you in some mythical never-never land? It would be my pleasure!"

"Mine, too," he assured her. "With you by my side, I'd go willingly. But first I have a battle to fight—and to win. So ante up, deal me in—and prepare to lose."

With that he stepped back and for the first time in what seemed like hours, Jordan took a breath. Her jaw burned from his touch, while fury burned within—fury mixed with confusion. A picture of his fingers stroking the plump red tomatoes flashed through her mind, adding to her confusion and banking her anger. She'd been right. His touch truly was exquisite....

She struggled to spark her anger anew, fearful of the strange emotions sweeping through her. She didn't want to feel this way about Rainer. Dangerous didn't begin to describe what such a feeling would be. He wasn't interested in romancing her. He wanted something much more—something she'd fight tooth, nail and big left toe to keep him from having.

"I think you should leave," she said in a low voice.

"And I think we should find your uncle and get down to business. Where's he hiding?"

She hopped off the watermelon bin. "You have a very abrasive way of doing business. I'll assume your family's produce markets are successful in spite of you, not thanks to you."

His expression was amused once more. "Assume anything you want. It's to my advantage to have an opponent underestimate me."

One thing she'd never do was underestimate this man. He'd shown her all too thoroughly just how much charm—and ruthlessness—he had. He'd revealed as much at the wholesale market. And then, in case she'd misunderstood, he'd proved it again in her own store. Uncle Cletus's store, she corrected herself grimly. It wouldn't do to forget that small, though pertinent, detail.

"Uncle Cletus isn't hiding anywhere. He's in the back, probably playing checkers with Walker."

A single eyebrow shot up. "He plays while you work? Curious setup."

"Uncle Cletus works very hard," she leapt instantly to her only relative's defense. "He isn't a young man anymore, and what with his stroke . . ." She trailed off, shrugging.

"Then perhaps he'll find my proposal of greater interest than I thought," Rainer said with satisfaction.

Jordan hesitated. He moved as though to head for the back of the store, and she put a resisting hand on his arm. "Wait." She licked her lips. "Please—" Lord, how the word came hard to her tongue. "Could you tell me what this is about? What do you intend to . . . propose?"

His gaze softened. "I think you know already, Jordan. Don't make it any harder on yourself than necessary. Come on. I know all about family businesses. And since, as you've so rightly reminded me, this is a family business, you should be there."

As she'd predicted, they found Uncle Cletus in the back with Walker. This time mangoes and kiwifruit littered their checkerboard, the game once again in progress. Jordan went to tap her uncle on the shoulder, but Rainer caught her hand, drawing her off to one side.

"We'll let them finish," he whispered and lowered himself onto a nearby stool. He became instantly absorbed in the progress of the game.

Jordan sat perched on the edge of a lunchroom chair. Why the delay? she wondered uneasily. Why didn't he get on with it? Stretching out the wait like this was pure agony. Perplexed, she glanced at him.

He seemed totally relaxed, as though he had all the time in the world. His fingers were templed beneath his chin, his arms resting on his knees. A lock of curly white-gold hair lay across his furrowed brow and she knew a moment's regret for the might-have-beens.

An attraction existed between them; honesty forced her to admit it. If circumstances had been different, she would have enjoyed exploring that attraction. She sighed, acknowledging the impossibility of it all. Even if Rainer hadn't taken such an adversarial position, the produce business didn't leave her much time for a social life.

She glanced his way again, sensing his growing tension. Curious, she studied him, realizing in dismay that he'd focused his full attention on her uncle. What was he up to?

It hit her like a class-five hurricane. He observed Uncle Cletus in order to analyze his moves and method of play. Rainer wasn't interested in the game; he was interested in evaluating her uncle! Just as he'd spent the morning watching her, figuring her out, now he watched her uncle, figuring out an angle to use against him.

Her eyes widened. An angle. Good grief—precisely what she always did. She sized up the competition, figured out an angle and moved in for the kill. Of course she'd always thought of it in slightly different terms. She'd get a general impression of her customers, figure out their needs and try to give them what they wanted. Her angles were...nicer, rounder, smoother. Whereas Rainer's were all sharp points and rough edges. But what gorgeous points and edges!

The game ended rapidly, but then, it always did. The only thing more certain than her uncle's winning a checker match was the chance of rain in a Seattle forecast.

"Walker," she said, "Andy needs some help sorting the oranges." Her uncle's friend took one look at Rainer and beat a hasty retreat. Jordan crossed to her uncle's side and put a gentle hand on his shoulder. "Mr. Thorsen wants to talk to us—about Cornucopia."

Uncle Cletus appeared startled—and dismayed—to find the man in question seated behind him.

"Make it Rainer," the younger man said and stood up, approaching with hand outstretched.

Cletus looked at it as he might a coiled rattlesnake and reluctantly stuck his gnarled hand into harm's way. "Since we're being sociable, call me Cletus," he muttered less than graciously.

"My father says he knew you and your brother years ago."

This seemed to cheer Cletus some. "Quite right. The community was smaller back then, more tight knit. In those days you knew everybody in the business. Not like now. Your father, Jake and I even socialized on occasion. I guess you could say we were the next best thing to kin." He gave a weak chuckle. "Welcome to the family, my boy."

A smile crept across Rainer's mouth. "Thanks."

"Nice of your pop to send you over to do the neighborly thing," Cletus said a trifle nervously. "How's Alaric feeling these days?"

"Just fine, thank you. He's looking forward to his sixtieth birthday this month."

Cletus shook his head. "Amazing how the years go by. My own sixtieth wasn't all that long ago." He stood up with a gusty sigh. "Well, son, it's been delightful to meet you. Just delightful. You tell your pop I'll try and stop by one of these days." He looked hopeful. "I guess you have to leave now?"

Jordan shut her eyes and let out a tiny groan.

"Not quite yet," Rainer said.

Cletus fell back into his chair. "No?"

"No."

"Uncle Cletus," Jordan began, only to be silenced by a stern look from Rainer.

He returned to his seat on the stool, his posture relaxed, casual even. It didn't fool her one tiny bit. She knew determination when she saw it—and this man positively screamed determination. "You received a letter from us a few months ago. Perhaps you recall?"

The older man's eyes shifted evasively. "Can't say that I do."

"Uncle Cletus?" Jordan stared at him in sudden suspicion. Rainer's information was unexpected and unwelcome. "What's he talking about?"

Rainer cut in. "Since your uncle didn't receive the letter, I'm sure he doesn't know. I do. Our letter outlined a proposition we wanted your uncle to evaluate." His gaze was cool and direct, and vaguely threatening. "Thorsen Produce is looking to expand.... Realizing this has always been Cornucopia's turf and realizing how . . . close the two families have been all these years—"

Jordan couldn't resist a small unladylike snort.

"Gesundheit. As I was saying, considering the close family ties, we wouldn't want Cornucopia to feel any loss due to our expansion."

"Why, thank you." Uncle Cletus beamed. "I'm sure Canada will be delighted to have a Thorsen Produce Market."

"No doubt." Nor was there any doubt about the irony in Rainer's voice. "Unfortunately we were thinking about Seattle's northern suburbs—say, Queen Anne Hill or Magnolia or even Blue Ridge."

Cletus frowned. "That's getting a mite close, son. I mean, there's such a thing as being too neighborly." Jordan gave his shoulder a comforting squeeze. Absently he patted her hand.

"I couldn't agree more," Rainer allowed, glancing from one to the other. "That's why we want to make you a small proposition. A . . . lucrative proposition, if you will."

The older man perked up at that. "Lucrative?"

"Quite."

Jordan wondered if her uncle heard the derision in Rainer's tone as clearly as she did. So he thought her uncle could be bought, did he? He'd soon learn differently. You couldn't put a price on family, and that was precisely what Cornucopia was—family.

"We'd like to buy Cornucopia from you."

"Buy Cornucopia! How dare you!" Cletus thundered.

Jordan wanted to cheer. *Way to go. You tell him!* She kept her hand on his shoulder, the touch one of restraint now, rather than comfort. She shot Rainer a triumphant grin.

"We're prepared to pay generously."

Cletus slammed his fist onto the checkerboard crate, narrowly missing a mango. "You can't put a price on a man's blood and sweat. You insult me!" He drew a deep breath. "Just out of curiosity, how much are you prepared to insult me with?"

Rainer mentioned a figure that left Jordan more than a little stunned. She turned a concerned gaze on Cletus. She wasn't feeling quite so cocky anymore. It was a lot of money. A whole lot of money.

The breath Cletus drew this time was shaky. "That's quite an insult," he muttered, then rallied. "You can't have Cornucopia for any price." He made the statement with quiet dignity. "This store was my father's before it was mine. I promised it would be Jordan's when I retire to my chicken ranch in New Mexico."

"Arizona."

"Exactly." Cletus grabbed Jordan's hand and squeezed it. "I'm sure you understand the importance of family in these matters."

Rainer inclined his head. "I do. I also understand the importance of business." He eyed them both, his gaze wintry. "Be forewarned. We're expanding northward. You can bow to the inevitable, take what you can and head for your chicken ranch, or—" he paused, his ruthlessness hiding every scrap of charm "—or you can lose it all."

"You can't be serious!" Jordan protested. "Are you threatening to put Cornucopia out of business?"

"Promising. I don't make—"

"Threats. I remember, you make promises," she said, a sarcastic edge creeping into her voice. "It's impossible to break Cornucopia. We'll fight you up and down, inside and out and back and forth, if necessary. The whole community will fight you!"

"Good." He grinned. "There's only one thing a Thorsen does better than fighting."

She knew she'd regret asking, but couldn't resist. "What's that?"

"Winning." He stood. "I believe my business here is completed. For today." He held out his hand to Uncle Cletus—a hand the older man pointedly ignored. Rainer dropped his arm to his side and glanced at Jordan. "See me out?"

She smiled tauntingly. "Afraid you'll get lost?" Then she sighed, "All right, come on."

When they reached the front door Rainer turned, catching her arm in a light grip. "I know this is difficult for you, but you need to be realistic. You can't win this fight."

Jordan pulled away from his touch. She couldn't afford to be affected in that way. Not now. Not with so much at stake. "We'll see," was all she said.

He took a final look around. "You own the building, as well as the business, don't you?"

He had to know that already, otherwise he wouldn't have made such a generous offer. Perplexed, she nodded. "Why?"

"Would you believe idle curiosity?"

"No."

He chuckled. "Smart lady. It's a fine building you have here. Almost as fine as the one they're constructing across the street."

She froze, sensing danger. "You're familiar with that project?"

"I better be. It's my building they're raising. Looks like we're going to be neighbors after all." And with that he left.

Jordan tried to convince herself that things weren't as disastrous as they seemed—which took a lot of convincing and the rest of the day.

A WEEK AND A HALF later, Jordan stood by her truck outside Constantine's Wholesale Market. Her frustration had finally reached unbearable levels. It was ten days since Rainer had appeared in her life. Ten days since he'd issued his ominous threats and warnings—ten days of silence.

And during that time she'd gone through the full emotional spectrum—anger, annoyance, concern and finally fear. Didn't he realize how worried she'd be? Or was that the whole idea? She wished he'd just do something and get it over with.

Determined to take some action of her own, she entered the warehouse and gazed toward the back at the offices on the second story. Large windows, some ajar, others tightly closed, overlooked the cavernous main floor where she stood. Andrea's, she noted, were open. Good.

She'd told her friend about the Thorsens' interest in Cornucopia. Perhaps there would be some much-needed information by now. Anything was better than living in a vacuum. And if nothing else, she could count on receiving one of Andrea's special pep talks—each guaranteed to find the bright side to even the worst disaster.

Andrea's door opened before Jordan had a chance to knock. "Oh, you're here," the tall blonde said with a rather weary smile. "I was about to come and get you. We need to talk."

Jordan grinned. "I'd hoped you'd say that."

She entered the room, shoved a stack of receipts off the chair and sat down across from her friend's desk. It always amused her to come here. A very clever businesswoman, Andrea seemed to thrive on chaos. Papers, invoices and produce manuals littered every inch of her office. Yet she could always find anything she needed at a moment's notice. Today, though, she seemed distracted and tense.

Jordan frowned. Now that she really looked, she realized Andrea had lost weight. And there was a new vulnerability in her friend's expressive dark eyes, the sparkling liveliness dimmed. There was no sign of the cheerful optimism that made her friend so special. "Is something wrong?" she asked, quick to put her own worries aside.

Andrea shrugged. "You know how this place gets sometimes. It's nothing I can't handle." She fumbled for some papers, her tone deliberately businesslike, almost offputting. "Listen, I've done some checking. Those threats Rainer made weren't idle ones. The Thorsens are serious about expanding."

Jordan dismissed the Thorsens with a wave of her hand. "Forget about that for now. Andrea, I know something's wrong. What—"

"You can't forget about it!" the blonde broke in sharply, her voice rising. "You don't know the Thorsens or their methods. I do. They're ruthless. They'll do anything and everything to get what they want. Believe me, I know."

The passion of her words seemed to hang between them. As though aware of how much she'd given away, Andrea leaned back and shut her eyes.

"How do you know?" Jordan asked gently. "How do you know so much about the Thorsens?"

Obviously she'd hit a nerve, for Andrea spun out of her chair and paced to the windows overlooking the warehouse floor. "I know because...because I was engaged—very briefly—to Rainer's brother, Thor," she admitted in a pained voice.

"You what?" Jordan stared in confusion. "When was this? You never mentioned an engagement before."

"It didn't seem worth mentioning, considering how quickly it ended." She turned around to face Jordan and sighed. "Last month—remember me raving about the wonderful man I'd met?"

Recollection returned. "You called him your thunder god." The pieces fell into place and she groaned, making the connection. "*Thor* Thorsen. *He's* the one you were so crazy about?"

Andrea nodded. Tears sparkled in her eyes, but her smile held defiance. "I fell in love with him. He fell in love with a lucrative contract my father offered. Unfortunately I didn't hear about it until after he'd proposed and I'd accepted. End of engagement, end of story. You'll understand why I didn't call you and go into all the thrilling details."

A memory stirred and Jordan heard again Terry's caustic words. "If it meant getting the Thorsens' business, the old man would sell his own daughter. Hell, he'd *give* her away." Is that what he'd been referring to, the aborted engagement? Did *everyone* know what had happened? Poor Andrea!

"So now you understand why I'm quite serious when I say the Thorsens are ruthless," Andrea continued. "Personal experience, as it were. But enough about me. Let's deal with your problem. Did you know Rainer's here today?"

Her words were more than unwelcome, and Jordan shifted uneasily in her chair. "No. You think it's related to Cornucopia, don't you?" At her friend's grim nod, she asked, "What do you think he'll do?"

Andrea thought for a minute. "I'm certain he'll weigh all his options before he acts. But there is one thing you can count on. If a Thorsen told you he plans to take over the north end market, then that's precisely what he'll do. If he said he's going to win no matter what, bank money on it, he'll win."

"How?" Jordan demanded in a tight voice.

Her friend took a deep breath. "I can only tell you what they've done before. One time the Thorsens wanted to acquire a market in White Center owned by an old man named Leo Goldbrick. The Thorsens moved in, and before you could blink, they'd forced Leo out."

"Forced him out? How?"

"They set up in competition—right across the street. They undercut all his prices and he never stood a chance." She shoved a hand through her curls, her dark brown eyes reflecting her distress. "When you have a couple of dozen stores, each one making huge profits, you can afford to carry a loser for a few months."

"They operated at a loss until he was forced out?"

"Got it in one."

Jordan sat in stunned silence, remembering Rainer pointing to the site under construction across from Cornucopia. He owned that building. He could put his own market in there, set himself up in direct competition. How long would it take before he forced Cornucopia out of business? Longer than Leo Goldbrick, she knew. But the end result would be the same.

She stiffened her back. "The community wouldn't tolerate it," she maintained stoutly. "And we won't sell."

"Look, Jordan." Andrea gazed at her intently, her voice low and earnest. "You'd better know their options. If you refuse to sell, and if it isn't economical to try and force you out like they did Leo, then they'll put markets in all around you, stealing away your business bit by bit. Hemming you in might not be a fast death, but it will be a death nonetheless. Can you handle that possibility?"

Jordan's gray eyes turned somber. "I'll have to. We'll need to anticipate their moves and counter them. The one thing they won't have considered is the community we service."

"Why is that a factor?"

A grin eased across her lips. "It's different from what they're used to. The neighborhood around us has two types, the older mostly Norwegian set, and the younger upwardly mobile set."

"The yuppies," Andrea said dryly.

Jordan laughed. "The yuppies. Fortunately for us, both groups seem to value the same thing—family and tradition. They won't shop at one of the Thorsen's sterile impersonal markets as long as Cornucopia exists."

Her friend looked encouraged. "Do you think so? There's a lot riding on that assumption."

"Which is why I'd better be right." And why she'd better have correctly understood the requirements of the community they served. If ever she counted on her expertise at figuring out the angles, it was now. And she prayed it wouldn't let her down.

JORDAN LEFT Andrea's office feeling hopeful for the first time since laying eyes on Rainer Thorsen. Until this moment, she'd run scared. Which was undoubtedly his intention. He wanted to keep her off kilter—have her reacting without thinking. Well, all that would change. He was clever, she'd give him that. But if she worked at it, she could find a way around clever.

Thanks to Andrea, she now knew Rainer's options. She also knew how ruthless the Thorsens could be. The knowledge gave her a number of choices. She liked that—being able to try one thing, and if it didn't work, switching instantly to something else. It meant she could plan ahead, figure out in advance how to counter each of his moves. Not that it would be easy. She knew better than that. But with Cornucopia at stake, she'd do whatever it took to win.

The first and most important thing was to get the community—knowingly or not—behind the market. That would spike Rainer's guns. That would—

"Umph!" She bounced off rock-solid muscle, the breath knocked clean out of her lungs.

"Hey, find a door, would you?" Rainer said in greeting. "It's a lot easier than trying to walk through walls." He cocked his head. "You look determined this morning."

"Thanks." She lifted her chin and met his gaze dead on. "I feel determined."

He peered down at her, his fingers brushing boldly against her cheek. "No storm clouds today I see. Your eyes tell me it's clear with sunny blue skies."

This time she didn't flinch at his touch. Instead a shiver caught her by surprise. His hands *were* pure magic. Each time he touched her, she found herself wanting the sensation to go on and on. As though picking up on her nonverbal cues, he reached out again, feathering a callused finger from her cheekbone to her chin.

"They're changing," he murmured. "It's like watching a cloud move across the surface of a lake."

"Stop it," she whispered. "This isn't the time or the place."

His voice dropped a notch. "Tell me the time and place, and I'll be there."

Jordan shook her head. "You know that's impossible." Then reality set in and with it an awareness of how much she'd given away. So he'd found an angle she hadn't anticipated, after all. The man was as beautiful as an angel, and as crafty as the devil. "You can't get Cornucopia that way," she informed him with cool pride. "I can't be bought any more than my uncle."

That deep rich laugh of his started rumbling in his chest. "I know. If that way led to Cornucopia, it would be mine already."

She gave a shocked exclamation and stepped back from him, anger replacing captivation. Andrea was right. The Thorsens really would try anything to get what they wanted. "Dream on."

His laughter died. "Deny it if you will, but before you ever laid eyes on me, you were aware of my presence. That had nothing to do with Cornucopia or the Thorsen name or what stands between us. It had to do with a man and a woman and the instinctive course nature takes. It's a course not easily changed."

"Don't bet on it."

"Bold words," he mocked her. "Fighting words. Shall I take them as a challenge?"

She sighed. "Don't you always?"

He rubbed a hand across his square-cut jaw. "I do, don't I?" There was laughter in the green depth of his eyes. "Challenge is good. Challenge works for me. And since the gauntlet's been thrown... Very well, I accept."

The first hint of alarm touched her. "Accept what? Hey, don't start that again. I didn't throw anything. I wouldn't know a gauntlet if it wore ribbons and sang opera."

He didn't seem to hear. "This will be even better than Cornucopia. Yes. I like this."

Jordan shook her head, backing away from him. "Mister, you're crazy. And I'm even crazier to stand here listening to you. I don't know what sort of challenge you think I issued, but you can forget it."

What did she mean, what sort of challenge? She'd been fully aware of the sexual undertones in their bantering. That sort of contest was as old as time. As old as Eve tempting Adam. But if she was smart, she wouldn't tempt *this* man. Because Vikings took—and she was darned if he'd take her.

"It's not good policy to show fear to your enemy," he informed her, perfectly serious. "And it's an even worse policy for a woman to show she fears a man. It brings out the hunting instinct."

"Climb down out of your tree, Tarzan. I'm not playing Jane, so forget it."

"Jord," he said reflectively. "Norse for mother earth. There is something elemental about you. Rainer. Norse for warrior." He stepped closer. "I always thought the meaning of names useless information. Until now. Now I find it rather fitting. What do you think?"

"I think I'm out of here." She turned her back on him and strode off.

He came after her. Catching her by the arm, he pulled her to a stop. "Wait." She yanked her arm free and he stepped away, giving her room. "I'm sorry, Jordan. I didn't mean to frighten you."

"You didn't," she said, ready to deny the truth with her dying breath.

By his expression, denying anything would be a waste of both time and energy. He offered her a soothing smile. "This isn't what I wanted to talk to you about. I wanted to ask a favor."

"You have a funny way of going about it."

A corner of his mouth curled upward in wry acknowledgment. "True. Still, I'd like to invite you to come with me tomorrow to visit some of the Thorsen markets."

Jordan stared at him in confusion, his offer taking her by surprise. "Why?"

"To prove the futility of your resistance."

Her confusion turned to disbelief. "How will showing me around your stores prove that our resistance is futile?"

He chose his words with care. "Look, I know that you run Cornucopia, not your uncle. If you pressed him to sell, he'd probably sell. Perhaps if you see our stores, see how strong our position is, you'll realize that selling is the best possible choice. In fact, it's the only choice."

That made her mad. "Let me tell you a thing or two about the choices I have—" She brought herself up short, her eyes narrowing.

No. She wouldn't say something she'd regret later. If she alienated him at this stage, she'd lose valuable insight into his motives. So far, he'd been very frank about what he wanted. He'd also been very frank about his attraction to her. Why not use that? It couldn't hurt to get to know the enemy and spot any possible weaknesses. In fact, she'd be a fool if she didn't.

"Okay, you're on," she said with renewed calm. "Pick me up tomorrow at nine and we'll visit the Thorsen markets." *And long may you live to regret it.*

CHAPTER FOUR

"CONSORTING with the enemy! That's what I call it!"

Jordan sighed. "Uncle Cletus, I'm not consorting with the enemy, I'm—"

The older man shook his head. "It's a sad, sad day when my only remaining kin, my own dear sweet niece, would desert her family for the enemy camp."

"Sad," Walker said, adding his two cents' worth.

Jordan and Cletus both turned and glared at the man. With a mumbled excuse he wandered over to the broccoli display.

Uncle Cletus practically wrung his hands. "Your Grandpa Joe is turning in his grave, weeping tears from heaven above."

"That's rain," she informed him dryly. "It does that a lot around here." She peeked at her watch, dismayed at how relentlessly the hands moved toward nine. If they didn't finish this discussion and get the morning's work done, she'd be late. "Uncle Cletus, do you want to sell Cornucopia?"

He drew himself up. "How could you ask such a question?"

"But do you?"

"Of course I don't. Why would you think such a thing?"

"Are you sure?" Jordan probed further. "The Thorsens are offering a lot of money. It's more than enough for you to retire on. You could be in Arizona before winter comes, have your chicken ranch, relax and enjoy the sunshine.''

His face fell. ''You'd rather I sell? I thought you loved Cornucopia.''

''I do. But we're talking about you and your needs right now.''

Cletus took her hands in his. His blue-gray eyes, so like her own, peered down with unusual intensity. ''My dear, the Roberts *are* Cornucopia. For nigh on fifty years this business has been our pride and joy, despite the struggle of the past ten. Perhaps I've been selfish, allowing an old man's dream to keep you tied when you'd rather be free.''

Tears misted her vision. She hadn't cried in so long she thought she'd forgotten how. It would appear she remembered. ''Uncle Cletus, I love Cornucopia. I love it almost as much as I love you. I don't want you to sell....'' She stumbled to a halt.

This wasn't the way she'd planned the conversation. How like him to put her wishes before his own. But she had to know how *he* felt. He shouldn't keep the store because of some outdated obligation. If they were to fight the Thorsens and win, they'd both have to work toward the same goal. It couldn't be just for her.

He smiled tenderly, as though understanding her thoughts. ''We're in this together, Jordan. We're a team. Of course I won't sell out. What would happen to you?''

''You can't worry about me,'' she declared passionately. ''I'm a survivor—you know that. I'll get another job, find a new obsession.'' She looked at him, filled with uncertainty. ''Are you sure you want to keep Cornucopia, Uncle Cletus?''

He gave an emphatic nod. ''Positive. And you?''

''It's a fight to the death.''

His former lament returned. "Then why are you going with Thorsen today?"

She laughed. "Would you believe because he asked me? And," she hastened to add, "for a little cloak-and-dagger."

The statement clearly intrigued him, stopping his lamentation mid-lament. "Spying?" His bushy eyebrows shot up and he scratched the bald spot on top of his head. "Spying! Jordan, you're brilliant."

She lowered her eyes modestly. "Tell me more."

"Yes. Yes. You could have something here." He rubbed his hands together, and Jordan almost laughed aloud, enjoying his enthusiasm. "You can figure out what the man's up to, use your feminine wiles. Be a regular Mata—" He stopped abruptly.

She giggled at his horrified expression, asking innocently, "Mata Hari?"

He stared at her as though seeing her for the first time and wagged his finger in her direction. "You dare and I'll turn you over my knee. How old are you, anyway?" he demanded suspiciously.

She struggled to keep a straight face. "Twenty-four last week. Don't you remember?"

Cletus shook his head in dismay. "If your father were alive, he'd lock you up and throw away the key. You're too pretty for your own good. No wonder that man's come sniffing around here."

"Uncle Cletus!" Jordan exclaimed.

An obstinate look darkened his features. "In fact, I've changed my mind about this whole business. He's too good-looking. And big, and strong, and…and blond! *I'll* go with him. He can show me around the Thorsen markets, instead." He brightened as an idea occurred to him. "On the other hand, maybe he isn't after Cornucopia at all. Maybe it's you he's after." The frown returned. "I'm not sure which is worse."

If only he *were* after her, the wistful thought popped into her head. If only Cornucopia didn't stand between them. But since it did and since he wanted the store... She'd never be certain if he romanced her to get his hands on the market or for herself. After all, look what happened to Andrea when she'd gotten involved with a Thorsen. Ruthlessly Jordan thrust the thought aside to be considered and mulled over when she had the time.

"You're reading too much into this, Uncle Cletus. I can guarantee it's the store Rainer wants, not me," she said firmly. "He thinks by showing me around Thorsen's, he'll change my mind and we'll hand him the store on a silver platter. He's wrong—he just doesn't know it yet."

Cletus wasn't convinced. "He's very good-looking."

"I haven't noticed," she lied without compunction. "My only concern is to get this man out of our lives. Permanently. I don't think we should let this opportunity slip by. Why don't *I* go with him." Lord, she sounded sanctimonious. She couldn't believe Uncle Cletus would fall for this.

But she could see him wavering. "We need a plan to defeat them," she said to drive home her point. "Getting the inside scoop could give us that plan."

"I guess." He relented, giving her a hug. "But you be careful. Don't get hurt."

Those sounded like famous last words, she thought uneasily. Or rather, infamous last words. She remembered again the feel of Rainer's finger on her cheek and shivered. How could she possibly protect Cornucopia when she couldn't even protect herself? She groaned inwardly. For crying out loud. Was she defeated already? Where was her backbone? Where was her spunk? Hiding with her courage, that was where.

"Hey, Jordan," Michelle's voice interrupted. "The customers are banging on the door. It's after nine. What should I do?"

Jordan shut her eyes. How could she possibly leave this place alone for a whole day? It would be a heap of rubble before the sun set. "Try opening the door," she suggested in a gentle voice. "I've found that usually works best."

Michelle's eyes widened. "Oops. I should have thought of that."

Jordan bit her tongue before the words dancing on the tip could escape. "Forget it, Michelle. I'll be there in a minute. Key in the registers instead, okay?" Obediently the younger girl trotted off. Jordan glanced at her uncle, and the two of them, unable to resist, burst out laughing. "I can't believe I'm standing around when I haven't even done the sign changes," she said ruefully.

"No problem. I'll do them," Cletus volunteered. "You never let me help with the signs. And you know how much I like doing them."

"Are you sure?" She couldn't keep the doubt from her voice. She'd had previous experience with Uncle Cletus's "help," and it was something she could live without repeating.

"Don't you think I can?" Her uncle's tone reflected his hurt.

"Of course I do. It's just..." She gave up. "The list is on the lunchroom table. There're only three items you need to change today, and I've circled the new prices."

"You'd think I'd never changed a sign before," he grumbled, stalking out of the back area.

Jordan sighed. That was precisely the problem. He had done them before, and a bigger mess she'd never seen. Oh, well, she'd have to risk it.

Rainer arrived just as she unlocked the front door. "Running a little late?" he asked. "Not good for business, you know."

"On the contrary. It makes them so eager to get in, they buy twice as much. Are we going to waste time exchanging insults, or are we leaving?"

He pretended to think about it. "Exchanging insults with you is tempting," he teased. "However, I think we'd better go."

Cletus came up to stand next to her, his expression reminiscent of a dog guarding a bone. "You watch him," he whispered loud enough to guarantee Rainer heard.

"Every second," she promised. "You won't forget to do up those signs for me? You can handle it?"

"Of course I can handle it," her uncle said in a wounded voice. "I'm not exactly new at all this, you know."

Jordan felt repentant. "No. I'm sorry. See you later."

She gave his cheek a quick peck and turned to Rainer. Why did she suddenly feel she'd taken her life in her hands? Or rather, put it into his, she amended as he grasped her fingers and tugged her out the door.

They dashed through the rain to a sporty red convertible, with the top, she noted with relief, up. He opened the door for her, tucked her in and closed it, before sprinting around to the driver's side and climbing in.

She glanced at him curiously. "Where are we going?"

"I thought we'd head to our southernmost stores. They'll be the ones most like Cornucopia. Then we'll run over to my parents' house. Thor said he'd be there this afternoon and I want to introduce you to him."

"He's your brother, right?" she said, her mouth turning down. Recalling Andrea's revelations of the previous day, she wasn't too anxious to meet this particular Thorsen. An image of a ferocious man with bright red hair, a ruddy complexion and a fierce expression rose before her. She shuddered, finding she preferred white-blond hair, a golden tan and laughing green eyes.

He pulled skillfully out into traffic. "My *big* brother."

"Big brother?" she repeated in disbelief. He must jest. She struggled to imagine a bigger version of Rainer and failed. The man beside her was too unique to copy, let alone enlarge.

Rainer gave a deep sigh. "Yes. It's sad, but true. I'm the second born, not the first." He shot her a cocky grin. "My mother tells me that's why I fight so hard to win."

"Is it?"

"Not that I'll admit."

Jordan's lips twitched. "Just naturally feisty, are you?"

He looked affronted. "Men aren't feisty. At least, not in my neck of the woods. What can I say? I like to fight."

"And win," she finished for him.

He laughed. "That, too. Which isn't easy when I'm up against a black-haired stormy-eyed Valkyrie."

"I'm flattered. I think."

"You should be." He glanced at her. "You have a better description?"

She sat in silence for a minute. Then a small memory stirred within her, tugging at emotions she'd banked down for years. "My...my Grandpa Joe used to tease me about my looks," she found herself revealing.

"What did he say?" Rainer asked gently. When she didn't answer, he urged, "Tell me. I'd like to know."

"He'd say...he'd say I had hair blacker than an Arizona night, cheeks as red as cherry tomatoes and eyes as gray as a Seattle day." She gave a self-conscious laugh. "He grew up in Arizona. My dad and uncle were born there, as well. I suppose that's why Uncle Cletus wants to return."

"Your grandfather started Cornucopia?" He caught her nod out of the corner of his eye and asked, "What was he like?"

Memories came flooding back and seemed to tumble out of their own volition. "Grandpa was a big gruff man. I remember he could hoist a hundred-pound sack of spuds on each shoulder and not break a sweat. He'd toss me up in the air as though I weighed no more than a cotton ball." She laughed. "I guess to him I didn't. He used to call me his little alfalfa sprout." For the second time that day, tears glistened in her eyes. "Isn't that silly?"

If anything, his voice became even more gentle. "It sounds like someone who loved his granddaughter very much. My father calls my niece, Laura, cabbage head. For some reason, she loves it. Maybe because she instinctively understands how much Dad loves her." He glanced at Jordan. "How old were you when he died?"

"Five. He and my mother were killed in a car accident."

Rainer muttered an exclamation and swung the car over to the side of the road. He switched off the engine and turned to her, his eyes reflecting his regret. "Lord, Jordan, I'm sorry. I didn't realize."

She shook her head. "It was a long time ago and the things I recall are more flashes than actual memories. I know I take after my mother. She was small and dark, too." Jordan shrugged helplessly. "It usually comes back to me in the form of a certain scent or expression. Or I'll hear someone laugh and it'll evoke a feeling of déjà vu."

"And your father?" he probed carefully.

"There was an accident at work—with the truck—when I was fourteen." She managed a smile. "You should have been around then. You could have gotten Cornucopia for a song."

"Don't." His voice was rough. "How did you manage?"

"Uncle Cletus did the best he could, but he needed help. Things went downhill businesswise for a while until I could learn the ropes. But these past few years have been pretty good—despite the stroke Uncle Cletus had last summer."

He sat very still. "Someone told me you've been buying at Constantine's for ten years. You've been going down there since you were *fourteen?*"

She nodded. "Uncle Cletus and I would shop before school. I'd help him set up and then come in to lend a hand after my classes were through for the day. Once I graduated from high school, I took over the buying altogether."

"I don't believe this," he muttered.

"Why not?" She stared at him, puzzled. "I'm much better at it than my uncle. He does wonderful displays and keeps the store in great running order. But he used to annoy the salesmen because he'd—" She stopped abruptly.

"Talk to all the produce?" Rainer finished the sentence for her.

Jordan felt her skin grow warm. "Don't you dare say anything snide about my uncle," she warned. "I love him dearly. If he weren't so...so obsessed with produce, we wouldn't be as successful as we are today."

Rainer shook his head. "I disagree. But I won't dispute it with you." He looked at her curiously. "When do you have time for a social life?"

"I manage," she said stiffly.

"Right. Now pull the other one. I work in this business remember? I know what sort of hours are involved." She started to argue and he put a finger to her lips. "Before you say it, I enjoy a social life only because I have help. Good help."

She spoke around his index finger, tempted to give it a bite. "And I have Uncle Cletus."

"Precisely." He stared down at her, his gaze speculative. "If ever there was a damsel in need of rescuing, she sits before me. Shall I sweep down on my white charger and carry you off?"

"No," she said in a firm voice. "I am not Cinderella and I do not think of working at Cornucopia as a life of drudgery. If I did, I'd quit. Nice try, but I'm not buying."

"And I'm not selling. Cornucopia is a success for one reason and one reason only. And it isn't your Uncle Cletus. As for you..." He smiled teasingly. "Maybe you should know what you're missing before you dismiss it out of hand."

"Maybe I shouldn't." But maybe she would, especially if he insisted.

He insisted.

Slowly he reached for her, his hands sliding into her hair, holding her in a light embrace. His head lowered, blocking out the rain-splattered windshield, blocking out the pale gray morning, blocking out all sight and sound and thought. Then he kissed her.

The touch of his mouth was infinitely gentle, his lips moving with delicacy across hers, coaxing a response. She sensed his restraint and wondered if he recognized her inexperience. She didn't care. She'd always been a fast learner, and he, she suspected, was a skilled teacher. Curious, she allowed her lips to part beneath his.

She didn't quite know when her feelings changed. One minute she was in his arms, enjoying his kiss, and the next, she was in his arms desperate for his kiss. Desire erupted with the unexpectedness of a hail storm. She felt his heart drumming in concert with her own, and an urgency began to build, growing more and more insistent. Never before had a kiss shaken her quite so badly. Never before had she *needed* a kiss quite so badly.

Her control dissolved like sugar in water, and she began to tremble, a soft groan slipping from her lips to his. She'd made a tactical error, she realized then. She'd been a fool to think Rainer should teach her anything that involved mutual touching. Touching him was a mistake—no, it was a disaster.

Jordan yanked herself free of his arms and wriggled backward, her spine glued to the car door. She stared at him with wide eyes.

"Nice, wasn't it?" he asked with a lazy smile.

"Yeah. Sure." She cleared her throat. "Nice."

"We should do that more often," he murmured. "Makes all those fruits and vegetables pale by comparison."

She lifted her chin. "If you say so."

"I say so." He leaned closer, pinning her with his bright green gaze. "Honey, I could suck all day on a chili pepper and not come close to the kick I get from kissing you. I'd bet my last zucchini squash you felt the same way."

It took her a minute to digest that. "Translation?"

"There's more to life than produce." He started up the car engine and eased back into the traffic.

She turned her head and stared blindly out the window. He'd been right about one thing. She didn't have much time for a social life. She never had. Not that she'd consciously missed it—Cornucopia occupied all her time and attention. She'd worked hard to build up the family business, and thereby honor her parents' memory.

Cornucopia! Her mouth tightened as she realized how much she'd given away. Some spy she'd turned out to be. Show her a little attention, a little sympathy, give her a kiss or two and she'd talk her fool head off. If she wasn't careful, she'd find the store romanced right out from under her very nose.

She glanced at him uneasily, remembering yesterday's amorous challenge. If he'd taken their bantering seriously, he'd learned far too much about her from that kiss. Not that she regretted her lack of experience, she just wished he hadn't gained such a keen awareness of it. If she was any judge, the hunter was hot on the scent of the prey. And the prey was running scared!

It took them close to an hour to get to the first market; Thorsen's South, the huge sign over the store proclaimed. Located on a prominent corner of a thriving community, the exterior gleamed white in contrast to the dull gray day. Window boxes filled with red and pink geraniums decorated the outside of the large windows.

"I like that," Jordan exclaimed. "It gives the store a homey sort of touch."

"Which is the idea," Rainer said. "It brings in more customers."

She grimaced. "Don't spoil it. I want to think it's done because someone likes flowers, not as a deliberate ploy to attract customers."

Rainer's smile was tinged with irony. "You're not being realistic. We're in business to make money. If a few flowers will bring in more customers or encourage those customers to buy that little bit extra, then flowers there will be." He shot her a quick look. "I'm sure you do the same."

She thought of the walls of her store, most of them decorated with the artwork of her customers' children. There were also those framed photos of the early days, when Grandpa Joe and her mother and father had been alive, prominently displayed in their special corner. Had she done that, even subconsciously, in an attempt to increase sales?

She shook her head. No. She'd done it to give Cornucopia an added warmth, to make it feel more like a home than an impersonal store. She'd done it because Cornucopia *was* home, more so than the house she occupied with Uncle Cletus. That it pleased the customers and made their shop more popular was an added bonus. But it certainly hadn't been done with cold deliberation in order to bring in those customers.

"You're wrong," Jordan stated firmly. "And that's why you'll never succeed in bringing us down." She looked him square in the eye. "Our store has a heart. More, it has a soul, and that's something you can't generate from balance sheets or analyze on computer printouts."

Rainer rubbed a hand across his jaw. "So you think our stores lack soul. Well, come in and see for yourself. My sister and her husband run this particular market. I believe you'll eat those words, my fiery friend."

They got out of the car and entered the store. Instantly a ball of white fluff streaked toward them, followed by a flurry of blond pigtails. The fluff reached Rainer first.

"Whoa, Snowy. Give me a chance to get through the door." Rainer laughed, catching the cat in his arms. He shifted the white Persian to his shoulders and caught hold of the pigtails, which turned out to be a little girl, somewhere around five or six.

Jordan watched in fascination as Rainer swung the child high in his arms, nearly unseating the cat.

"Uncle Rainer, Uncle Rainer! Mommy said you'd come today."

"And here I am." He turned to Jordan. "This rambunctious young lady is my niece, Laura."

Jordan looked startled. "Not..."

"Cabbage head," he confirmed, with a teasing grin. "And this fur ball is Snowy." He set Laura on her feet and handed her the cat. "Off you two go before the health inspector hears we've got animals in the store."

Obediently the little girl carted the cat away. Rainer turned to Jordan, gesturing expansively with his arms. "Well, here it is. What do you think?"

Jordan looked around, admiring, despite herself, the clean bright interior. Everything shone either white or chrome—the floors, the metal counters and bins, even the walls. All the color in the store came from the produce, attractively displayed in neat rows and columns.

"It's lovely." Professional curiosity took over and she began to wander up and down the aisles, studying their arrangements and comparing prices and quality.

They'd done an excellent job, yet she felt a vague sense of disappointment. Despite what Rainer thought, they were still missing something. All right, maybe the store wasn't precisely soulless, but it lacked the warmth and charm of Cornucopia. This market remained . . . just a market.

If Thorsen's South was just a store, she soon learned that Rainer's sister, Brita, and her husband, Kevin, were much more than mere owners. Unlike the store, they were special, their personalities bright and attractive and friendly. Brita, whose coloring matched Rainer's, was surprisingly small and dainty. She greeted Jordan as though they were old friends and then ushered her up a flight of stairs in the back of the shop.

"We live in the apartment above," she explained. "We can sit and have a cup of tea and talk, while Rainer and Kevin deal with the business details." She opened the door to a comfortable-looking living room and led the way to the kitchen.

"Aren't you involved in that end of things?" Jordan asked, wondering about their setup.

Brita put a kettle of water on the electric burner. "You mean, am I the little woman who minds the register and can't add two and two without a calculator?" she guessed shrewdly.

"Open mouth, insert size sevens," Jordan muttered apologetically.

The young woman laughed, not unkindly. "In our family all we ever do discuss is business. So I'm happy to find any excuse for a break from it. No," she corrected herself instantly. "That's not true, and I wouldn't want to give you the wrong impression."

"You love it, don't you?"

Brita nodded. "Our family is very close, and since most of us are in the business in one capacity or another, it's natural there'd be a lot of shoptalk." Her eyes twinkled. "If there's two things Norwegians love, it's family and food. Working in this business gives us the best of both."

"I notice you each have Norse names..." Jordan struggled for a tactful way to phrase her question.

"You're wondering if we're big on Norwegian ancestry?" Brita smiled. "You haven't met Thor yet or you wouldn't ask. Yes, we take our heritage seriously. I'd have chosen a Scandinavian name for Laura, but Kevin put his foot down. Lord help whoever Rainer marries. It'll be Norse all the way."

Jordan's heart did a queer leap. She saw him again, scooping Laura up into his arms, his face alight with genuine pleasure and affection. He'd be that way with his own children. He had a natural affinity for them that surprised and delighted her. "Strange that he's not married yet, considering how he feels about family."

Brita shot her a knowing look, but all she said was, "He hasn't found the right woman. We'll know when he does."

She pulled mugs out of the cupboard and set them on the counter, dropping a tea bag in each.

Jordan resisted as long as she could. "How?" she asked fatalistically.

"He always said he'd stay single until he found an honest-to-goodness Valkyrie. That's a—"

"Warrior maiden. I know." Her brain went into overdrive as she analyzed the implication.

"Do you now," Brita murmured. "How interesting. And do you also know the legend behind the Valkyries?" Jordan shook her head. "They're actually Odin's maids. He's the Norse god who, according to legend, created the world. Whenever humans fought a battle, the Valkyries swooped down in all their armored glory. They determined which warriors were destined to fall in battle and carried off those who died bravely to join Odin in Valhalla, the Hall of the Slain."

Jordan was enthralled. "And?"

Brita wrinkled her nose, pouring steaming water into the mugs. "And the Valkyries waited on those fallen warriors, feeding them, bringing them drink—among other things. Mortal men considered it quite an honor to marry a Valkyrie. I think Rainer liked the tale because his name—"

"Means warrior. Yes. He told me." She frowned, pondering Brita's words. The Valkyries had the power of life or death over the warriors. Could that be why Rainer intended to marry a modern-day Valkyrie? Because she would have the power of life or death over his love? It was a romantic notion and made her see Rainer in a whole new light. Charming. Ruthless. And now romantic. The pieces made a very confusing—and intriguing—whole.

"So," the petite blonde said, handing Jordan a mug and changing the subject. "I understand you have a produce market, too. We literally live, breathe and eat this business, don't we?''

Jordan grinned. "You'd think I'd get tired of it, but ..." She shrugged. "Sometimes I think it's in the blood."

"I guess you'll get plenty of rest from it soon enough." Brita leaned a hip against the counter and sipped the hot tea. "What will you do when Cornucopia is sold?"

Jordan stared at her, stunned. Before she could disabuse the woman of her totally erroneous notion—and in no uncertain terms—Rainer's voice came from behind.

"Wrong question, sister dear," he said wryly. "The lady isn't convinced she wants to sell. That's the point of our visit."

"Oops." Brita turned an engaging grin in Jordan's direction. "Sorry. I didn't realize. Kevin gave me the impression it was in the bag."

"Did he?" Jordan glared challengingly at Rainer.

Brita laughed, not noticing anything amiss. "Let me warn you," she said lightly. "Rainer *always* gets what he wants. He never loses."

Jordan stiffened. She'd begun to get tired of hearing that. Very tired. "Then this will be a first," she said in a cold voice.

Brita's grin faded. She glanced from one to the other, and understanding dawned. To Jordan's disquiet, a hint of compassion showed in the light green eyes. "I'm sorry," she repeated.

This time her words weren't meant as an apology. This time they acknowledged the inevitability of Rainer's winning—and Jordan knew it.

CHAPTER FIVE

THE NEXT HOUR was sheer torture. Sitting and talking with Brita and Kevin as though nothing had happened strained Jordan's tolerance to the limit. At long last their time together ended. With cordial farewells, Rainer ushered her out of Thorsen's South and back into his car.

"I have the feeling your sister knows something I don't," Jordan said abruptly.

Rainer started the engine and glanced over at her, not attempting to put the car in gear. "She does."

He said it with a calmness and finality that made her want to shriek in protest. Instead, she strove to sound equally composed. "She thinks you're going to win, doesn't she?"

His voice didn't change inflection. "She knows me."

That didn't mean she was right, Jordan wanted to say. Lots of younger sisters idolized their older brothers. Again she saw that flash of sympathy in Brita's green eyes and winced. Okay. So she had a major fight ahead of her. That didn't come as any surprise.

Rainer set the car in motion and headed north toward Seattle. The sun peeked through the last of the storm clouds, and everything shone with a clean fresh-washed clarity. If only she could have such clarity in her own life. Thanks to the man at her side, things were about as clear as mud.

"So, where next?" she asked.

"Several fast stops at a number of our markets. Part of my job is to check with each store and see how things look. Basically what you did at Thorsen's South."

"What do you mean?"

"When you went through the store, didn't you compare prices and quality with Cornucopia?" She nodded, and he continued, "You looked at the size and types of displays, how well stocked each item was and how we'd chosen to arrange them. I'll bet you even peeked in the cooler."

"I couldn't resist," she admitted. "They do a good job. It's clean and attractive. The only problem I noticed—" She stopped, aware her comment might be misconstrued as criticism.

"Go on," he prompted.

Dare she be honest? Why not. He could take it. And if he couldn't? She shrugged. Too bad. "The traffic flow missed your back left corner. It's cut off from the rest of the store."

To her relief, Rainer seemed pleased by her observation. "Very good," he approved. "Kevin and I were just discussing that. They recently put in new refrigeration units and redesigned the store's layout to accommodate them."

"If they move the greens against the wall and build an island for the berries," she suggested diffidently, "that should take care of it."

He stopped at a red light and turned in his seat. Before she could discern his intention, he leaned over and kissed her. "We think alike, you and I," he said, his mouth inches away. "We should work together more often." His eyes darkened. "We should do this more often, too." And he kissed her again, his mouth hard and warm and demanding. She didn't resist. It didn't even occur to her. His kiss felt too good. Worse, it felt right.

A horn blaring from behind brought them both to their senses. With a muttered word of regret, Rainer drove on.

They stopped at four more markets and followed the same procedure at each. She and Rainer walked through the store, discussing the good points and bad. Each time he'd ask her opinion, and each time she felt more and more comfortable offering it.

To her chagrin she discovered that Rainer's relatives managed the Thorsen stores, his family, it would seem, as prolific as it was ruthless. Not only that, every one of them had heard of her and knew what Rainer wanted from her—and judging by the smiles and joking comments, they didn't think it was Cornucopia alone.

"Next stop, my parents' home," Rainer announced shortly after noon. Jordan wasn't sure whether to feel curious or wary. To her surprise, he drove them to Magnolia, a beautiful hilltop community just outside Seattle and within a stone's throw of Cornucopia.

"They've lived here for years," he explained, pulling into the driveway of a huge sprawling estate. "I thought you'd prefer meeting everyone in less businesslike surroundings."

Jordan looked out over the vast green lawn and at the dozens of children and adults milling about. "Are all these people relatives?" she asked, taken aback.

"Mostly. Cousins, aunts, uncles, with a number of employees thrown in for balance. Mom and Dad encourage everyone to visit Friday afternoons. We talk business and hash out problems. A lot of the kids spend the day at the stores with their parents, so this gives them an opportunity to run around and release pent-up energy."

"So many," she marveled, a hint of envy creeping into her voice. How she longed to be part of a family this size. Watching the enthusiastic crowd gave her a vague sensation of loss and regret.

"Come on and I'll introduce you around." He smiled down at her, a tender light in his eyes.

Did he suspect how she felt? After their conversation that morning, he must. "I'll never remember everybody," she warned.

"Don't try. When in doubt, just throw out a Norwegian name. You're bound to get at least one response."

She gave him a wry look. "That's presuming I know any Norwegian names."

His voice was a seductive murmur. "You know mine. That's all that counts." He pointed to a tall handsome woman. "There's my mother. Come on. You'll like her."

"Call me Sonja," the youthful hazel-eyed woman requested. "If you call me Mrs. Thorsen, you'll have at least a dozen women answering you." She gestured toward the back of the house. "There's some iced tea out on the patio. Why don't we sit there?"

Loungers, deck chairs and tables cluttered the patio, and a huge pitcher of iced tea rested on a long bar. Rainer took three glasses from a stack by the pitcher and filled them to the brim.

"Mint?" he asked Jordan. At her nod, he added a sprig and handed her the glass. "Don't let all the people overwhelm you. You'll get used to it in time," he said, accurately reading her dazed expression.

He sat down and took precisely one swallow of his drink before finding himself knee-deep in kids. "Come and play!" they urged, his laughing resistance ignored. They yanked on his arms until he gave Jordan a helpless shrug as though to say, "What can I do?" and leapt to his feet. He sprinted easily across the lawn, a pack of screeching youngsters giving chase.

Jordan watched from her lounger in fascination, impressed with his natural affinity with children—and at the way his large body moved with well-coordinated grace and power. When the breeze carried his deep laughter across the lawn, she felt a stab of envy, wishing again she could be part of such a huge loving group.

"I gather you don't have a big family," Sonja commented from beside her.

"Is it so obvious?" Jordan gave a rueful laugh. "Or did Rainer tell you about my background?"

"My son's been remarkably closemouthed about you. Your expression gave you away." She inclined her head toward Rainer. "He has a boyish quality about him that's very appealing, don't you think?"

Rainer, boyish? Jordan strove to offer an honest, though tactful response. She couldn't think of one. "No." She sighed. Perhaps Sonja appreciated honesty.

Apparently she did, for she laughed in genuine amusement. "So. You've run up against the Thorsen wall. All the men in this family have it."

"Wall?" Jordan questioned, interested.

Sonja nodded. "That's what I call their stubborn determined streak. You can't get over it, under it or around it. It's impregnable. Or so they think." She gave a wide mischievous smile. "Would you like to hear how I get through?"

A memory teased her. "Wait. You...find a door," Jordan said, suddenly remembering Rainer's laughing remark when she'd tried to run him down at the wholesale market.

Sonja stared at her in amazement. "He told you this?"

"One time, as a...a joke. I bumped into him and that's what he said."

"It's a family expression," the older woman explained. "I use it when the men get too hardheaded."

"When do we get too hardheaded?" came a deep voice from behind.

"You—all the time," Sonja scoffed. "Jordan, this mountain of a man is my oldest, Thor."

"Ms. Roberts," Thor said. He held out his hand, much as Rainer had at the end of their first meeting.

Tentatively, she slipped her fingers into his. So this was Andrea's thunder god. She'd have to readjust her preconceived image of a fierce ruddy giant.

His hair, instead of being the bright red of legend, gleamed tawny as a lion's pelt, a hint of auburn burnishing it. Rainer and his brother shared certain features—the determined chin and high strong cheekbones—but Thor's expression remained stern and closed, revealing none of the zest and humor that made Rainer so attractive.

"I'll relinquish you into Thor's capable hands," Sonja said unexpectedly. "As much as I love lazing around in the sun, dinner preparations come first."

And leave her all alone with this man? Forget it! Jordan knew a threat when she saw one. And Thor was a major threat. "I'd love to help," Jordan offered quickly. "What can—"

"No, no. I have more than enough women in my kitchen. Let Thor entertain you." Sonja slanted her son a teasing grin. "See if you can get him to smile."

Thor waited until his mother left, then turned in his chair, scrutinizing Jordan. She gave him back look for look, finding the intense blue color of his eyes far less appealing than Rainer's vivid green.

"My brother is right. He *has* found himself a Valkyrie." She didn't respond, and his scrutiny sharpened. "You prefer we skip the small talk? I agree. Let's cut to the bottom line."

She tensed in her seat, remembering Andrea's warnings about the Thorsens in general—and this man in particular. "Which is?"

"Which is the need to come to terms about Cornucopia."

Jordan leaned forward, determined to play the aggressor. "Am I supposed to simply agree to whatever terms you choose to offer, take your money and walk away from three generations' worth of work?" she asked. "Is that what *you* would do?"

"No," he admitted. "But you're not me."

"You're right." She glared at him. "What I am is a single woman, dependent on my family's business for survival. A survival you and Rainer threaten." Before he could respond, she added, "I know. I know. You two don't make threats. I've already heard that line. It loses its effectiveness with repetition."

"It shouldn't." The very mildness of his response made it all the more alarming. "You seem to have a misconception about this whole situation. You act as though we're doing something unscrupulous or underhanded, that we've wronged some innocent victim."

"And you haven't?"

"Not at all. Do you really believe we need Cornucopia?"

She stared at him in confusion. "You don't?"

He shook his head, a small smile of amusement playing about his broad mouth. "Not at all. We're offering you a very generous price for a store that will cease to exist within a year or two."

She couldn't believe it. "You're going to buy Cornucopia so that you can close it?"

"If we bought your store, it would become another Thorsen market. But if you refused to sell, we'd open markets all around you, and before long Cornucopia would be cut down to nothing."

"Why?" She could barely get the word around the frozen muscles of her jaw.

He inclined his head. "A fair question. You see, right now your store has a lock on the north end. We need to smash that lock—one way or another." His smile didn't reach the wintry blue of his eyes. "Take the money, Ms. Roberts. I'd rather be kind than cruel. But make no mistake, we intend to break your hold no matter what."

He'd repeated Andrea's words, almost verbatim. It would seem her friend knew this man all too well. Jordan turned her head away from him, her gaze settling almost instinctively on Rainer. He and the kids had progressed to a rough-and-tumble game of football. Part of her longed to leap to her feet and scream for him.

Once again she realized these were serious men. And they meant business. This was no game.

As though sensing her agitation, Rainer rose from beneath the pile of youthful bodies covering him and stared across at her. He stooped down and said something to the children, then loped toward her. She noticed again his easy grace, admiring, despite herself, his rugged build. His hair was damp with sweat, his chest rising and falling with his quickened breath. As he stepped onto the patio, she could smell the sweet scent of grass that clung to him.

He glanced at her for a brief moment, a question in his gaze, before turning to greet Thor. "I didn't see you arrive. Been here long?" He reached for his glass of tea, draining the icy beverage in one swallow.

"Long enough."

Rainer returned the glass to the table and lowered himself onto the edge of Jordan's lounger that was closest to his brother. For an insane moment she had the impression he sat there in order to protect her, putting himself between her and danger.

"I wanted to be here when you met Jordan." Beneath his surface congeniality, Rainer's voice held anger. At his brother? she wondered.

Thor shrugged. "You didn't miss much. I gave Jordan certain truths. Perhaps any further...discussions should be with her uncle, since he owns Cornucopia."

"Back off, big brother." There was real menace in Rainer's voice. "You're overstepping your boundaries."

Suddenly Jordan was sick of the whole situation. She'd had it with these Thorsen men and their not-so-subtle threats and their bickering and their...kisses? Was she tired of dealing with those, too? She'd have to be. She could live without Rainer's magic touch. Sure, it felt wonderful, incredible even. Sure, she felt as if she'd been to heaven and back, and every nerve in her body shrieked for more. But she could live without heaven. Couldn't she?

"I'd like to leave," she announced, jumping to her feet. If she hung around heaven too long, she might be tempted to stay.

After one swift searching look, Rainer stood up, not attempting to dissuade her. He spoke privately with Thor for a minute, and then took her arm and led her through the house. "We'll say goodbye to my mother before we leave."

"Of course." She even managed to sound sincere when she made her excuses. *I can handle this,* she decided miserably. *Living without heaven will be a snap.*

Sure it would.

Rainer waited until they were back in the car before starting his questions. "What did he say to you? Why are you running scared?"

"I'm not scared!" She turned her head away. "And Thor didn't say anything you haven't said already. At least, not much more."

"What else, Jordan?"

Not Valkyrie anymore, she noticed, with an unwanted rush of regret. Did she act as beaten as she felt? She sighed. "He explained why we can't win." She turned and met his compassionate gaze. "Don't get too excited. I'm not convinced. Yet."

If he picked up on how much she betrayed with her final qualifying word, he didn't show it. His eyes gleamed with gentle mockery. "You'd disappoint me if you were."

She lifted her chin in a gesture of defiance. "You don't see any white flags flying, do you?"

He chuckled and started the engine. "Not a one." He backed out of the driveway and headed away from Magnolia. They drove in silence, though it didn't seem uncomfortable. Within minutes they were approaching Cornucopia. "Where should I drop you off?"

"Home. It's the house behind the store." She'd check Cornucopia over later. She needed time alone. Time to think.

He pulled up in front of the house and parked. A huge marmalade tomcat jumped onto the hood of the car and Rainer's eyebrows shot upward. "What is that?" he demanded.

"That's Scratch. He's part cat, part mountain lion and owns this part of town."

"I guess." He dismissed the cat and turned to study her, concern reflected in his voice. "You look so...defeated."

"What do you want?" she asked. "A fight? Fine. Put 'em up. We'll duke it out."

"Tempting, but—" he shook his head "—I'll pass, thanks."

"Then what?" she demanded, shaken.

"You already know. I'm after Cornucopia, nothing will alter that. But I'd rather not destroy you in the process.

Change is inevitable. How you adapt to change is up to you."

"In other words, adapt or die? Never," she declared. A rush of fierce anger rose within her, jerking her from her lethargy. "I won't give in."

He reached for her, ignoring her attempts to evade his touch, and captured her chin in his hand. "I didn't bring you along today so we could fight." A tiny grin softened his mouth. "And though I enjoy our little battles, they aren't meant to wound. Don't keep battering yourself against me. I make a rough barrier. You'll hurt yourself."

She believed him. Like a human wall, everywhere she turned stood Rainer, cutting her off, wearing her down, straining her to the limits both emotionally and physically. She'd almost run out of angles. The threat to Cornucopia, a threat she'd once thought ridiculous, grew slowly, inevitably, more and more real.

His hand moved from her chin, his fingers sliding to cup the side of her face. "Relax," he urged. "Enjoy today. Tomorrow will take care of itself."

She shook her head, unable to dislodge his hand. "If I don't think of tomorrow, who will?"

Something flared deep in his eyes, the turbulent green darkening. "I will."

He eased her closer to him, a strange tension visible in the set of his jaw. His fingers slipped deep into her hair, tangling in the thick dark curls. He placed his free hand on her waist, his palm warm and heavy through her cotton shirt.

"If you'd let me," he murmured, "I'd take care of today and tomorrow and all the days after that." His mouth touched the corner of hers, tasting, nipping, inching along, until he finally staked full claim.

Jordan sighed, her lips parting, savoring the faint taste of mint tea on his breath. She slid her hands across his chest and then around his back. His grip on her waist shifted, his hands straying down to her hips.

The magic of his touch began again, first on her back, tripping along her spine, then his hand drifted to her side. She couldn't catch her breath. Her skin quivered beneath his fingers, and she clutched his shoulders, struggling for control.

"Jordan," he groaned into her mouth. "This is how we should always wage war. Here we both win."

She didn't want to hear his words, didn't want to think. She knew what he was—a warrior, his battles fought long and hard and relentlessly.

Even as the thought passed through her head, she could feel herself giving ground, surrendering to this man. She reveled in his strength and skill, exhilarating in the knowledge that she could arouse him just as thoroughly as he could her. It would seem she, too, had weapons.

I always win! His words came back to taunt her. But he wasn't the only winner in this contest.

Unless he gained Cornucopia.

The thought intruded on her euphoria. She remembered what had happened with the bananas. He hadn't lost that confrontation, because bananas weren't his ultimate objective. Cornucopia was. And now? Could his ultimate objective again be Cornucopia?

With a soft moan, she ended the kiss, turning her head when he sought to find her mouth again. She couldn't think straight. She couldn't even breathe properly. Nothing worked the way it should. Not her brain, not her nervous system . . . not her heart.

He frowned. "What's wrong? Look at me, Jordan. Talk to me."

"You know what's wrong," she whispered. "It's not bananas you want this time, either. Is it?"

He laughed, frustration edging the sound. "You're speaking Cletus-ese. Speak English."

She stared at him, feeling hauntingly alone. "Which do you want? Me or Cornucopia?"

He didn't hesitate for a moment. "Both."

"How do I know that? How do I know that I'm not like the bananas you claimed to want, that once you have Cornucopia, you won't..." She couldn't say the words.

"Drop you like a hot potato?"

"Don't be flip!"

He sighed. "You don't know. You'll have to trust me."

She thought of Thor and Andrea, and knew that Rainer asked the impossible. Carefully she moved toward the door, away from the warmth of his arms. "That's the problem. I don't trust you." His face darkened in anger and she shivered. She had choices to make that didn't allow her to take his feelings into consideration. She couldn't even take her own into consideration.

She looked at him. "I won't play games with you anymore," she announced. "No more challenges or battles or Norse myths and legends. I want you to leave Cornucopia alone. I want you to leave my uncle alone. But most of all, I want you to leave me alone."

He didn't say a word and she knew there were no words left to be said. She opened the car door and got out, slamming it closed. Only then did she realize she'd left a chunk of her heart in his keeping....

LATE THAT NIGHT, she walked through the store, restless and filled with an uncharacteristic dread. She looked around. How would her battle with the Thorsens change things? And what would happen to Cornucopia and Uncle Cletus should she misjudge any phase of this battle? She touched her double-sided nickels. It would take more than a coin trick to beat the Thorsens.

Thor, even more than Rainer, would be a merciless adversary, mainly because he didn't care about her or Uncle Cletus or, for that matter, Cornucopia. Though why she believed Rainer did—especially when she suspected his motives for kissing her—she didn't know.

She paused in front of the pictures of her parents and stared at their smiling faces. She'd tried so hard to follow in their footsteps. What, she wondered, would they have done in her place? How would they have tackled the Thorsens? Would they have continued to fight, or would they have bowed to the inevitable?

She stopped herself cold. Bowed to the inevitable? Her lips curved into a humorless smile. The Thorsens would be delighted to learn of the success of their tactics. One day in their company and she'd practically given up. The thought infuriated her. A lot.

"Jordan?" Her uncle's voice came from the far side of the store. "Are you there, honey?"

"Right here, Uncle Cletus."

He approached slowly, his brows raised in bewilderment. "What are you doing all alone in the dark? Is something wrong?" He frowned. "That Thorsen, did he . . ."

Jordan crossed to his side and put her arms around his shoulders, hugging him. "No, no. He didn't say or do anything that hasn't been said or done already." She pulled back and met his concerned gaze, giving him a gentle smile. "We need to talk."

Cletus released a gusty sigh. "I had a feeling you'd say that. Well, are we sunk?"

"Not yet." She shot him a piercing look. "This morning you said you wouldn't sell Cornucopia. You need to think about it and be certain that's what you want before we go any farther. I should warn you, they're very serious about all this."

"Hmph," he snorted. "They don't scare me."

"They should." She forced herself to speak dispassionately. "If you were smart, you'd take their money and run as fast and as far as you can. Straight to New Mexico and your chicken ranch."

"Arizona."

She nodded. "Exactly."

His eyes glittered with a hint of anger. "Do you honestly believe I'd strip away your heritage and leave you all alone? You know I wouldn't do that. We're family. We stand together."

"We may fall together."

He put a fatherly arm around her shoulders. "You're so pessimistic this evening. What's gotten into you?"

She groaned, relaxing into his arms. "It's not going to be an easy fight. The best I can tell, they have three choices and none of them are pretty. Rainer owns that building going in across the street, did I tell you that? One of his choices is to put in a competing market and drive us out of business."

"You mean he can try," Uncle Cletus said, "and fail."

"Another option is to buy us out," she continued. Her uncle didn't even dignify that with a reply. "Or finally, they can go around us, putting markets in Queen Anne Hill and Magnolia and Greenlake and Fremont. It would steal a lot of business from us. It might be ages before you could retire."

"You want me to sell, pumpkin?" he asked gently, using one of his childhood endearments. "If you do, just say the word and we're out of it."

Jordan shook her head. "There's a chance we can win." Her determination grew, and a slow grin crept across her mouth, banishing the grim lines. "And there's an even bigger chance we'll lose. How much of a gambler are you?"

He crushed her against him in a bear hug. "Roll the dice, girl, roll the dice. We haven't crapped out yet, and with a little peck on the cheek from Lady Luck, we'll hit us a jackpot."

"We're in this together, Uncle Cletus," Jordan assured him, returning his embrace. "Now we have to make some plans."

Uncle Cletus planted a kiss on her brow and released her. "Fire when ready."

"I want to start running weekly spots in the newspaper. We'll advertise one or two major loss leaders and see if we can't increase our customer base."

"Loss leaders?" he asked with a hint of alarm.

"You know," she was quick to explain, "we'll push strawberries or melons at cost and make it up on all the other goodies customers buy in addition."

"Well, if you think we should..."

"I do. We'll also push the 'family' angle for all it's worth, the tradition and heritage that makes Cornucopia so special." She snapped her fingers. "Maybe I can interest one of those newspaper types in running a story about us, go at it from a historical angle."

"I like the sound of that."

Jordan rubbed her hands together, warming to her theme. "If we can generate enough attention, it will help spike the Thorsens' guns when the time comes. I can just see the headlines—'Viking marauders pillage and plunder Mom 'n' Pop shop.' How does that grab you?"

Cletus chuckled. "Makes my blood boil. Think it'll rile up the natives?"

"It's sure to. Everyone loves an underdog. It's human nature—and a great angle. The Thorsens will look worse than...than..."

"Viking marauders?" he repeated back her words.

"Well, maybe not *that* bad. But close enough." She threw her arms around her uncle, giving him another fierce hug. "We can do this, can't we? We'll make it work."

"Was there ever any question?" her uncle said, mildly surprised. "You always figure something out. You've got more angles than a...than a spiral staircase."

Jordan blinked. "Uh—aren't those circular?"

Her uncle waved her comment aside. "You know what I mean. Why, if you set your mind to it, you could sell ovens to the Eskimos."

She sighed and linked her arm in his. "I suppose that would be easier than refrigerators. Come on. Let's head back to the house and draw up battle plans. The Thorsens won't know what hit 'em."

Or if they did, she sincerely hoped they wouldn't know what to do or how to do it.

CHAPTER SIX

THE NEXT MORNING, Jordan walked into Cornucopia and began her daily inspection. She glanced around and nodded to herself, pleased. Things didn't look too bad, considering she'd been gone all of Friday. With Saturday their busiest day, she wanted to be certain everything was perfect.

She'd missed seeing Rainer at the wholesale market that morning, and it galled her that she'd spent most of her time watching for him. Perhaps he didn't intend to use Constantine's after all. Not that it mattered. Goodness no. What did she care?

She grimaced. *Why* did she care, came closer to the truth. And she didn't think she could handle the answer.

The root table passed her inspection and she moved on to the fruits. She paused by the papayas and frowned at the sign advertising the price. That couldn't be right. She did some rapid math in her head, her frown deepening. The way things stood now, they were selling the papayas below cost.

Jordan closed her eyes. Uncle Cletus. He'd taken the responsibility for changing the prices yesterday. There had only been three, but...

She crossed to the cantaloupes and swore beneath her breath. They were mismarked, too. And the corn? To her relief, she found the price correct. Okay, it wasn't as bad as she'd initially thought. They'd only lost a little money on the mistakes—no serious damage done.

Swiftly she ripped down the signs over the papayas and cantaloupes and picked up the price sheets by each of the registers. Thank goodness she'd caught the errors. Poor Uncle Cletus. She smiled in genuine affection. He sincerely wanted to help. Numbers just weren't his strong point. Well, numbers were hers, which made for a good balance.

Setup progressed the same as any other day. By nine, things were still in a state of chaos: Andy and Leroy argued over the placement of the strawberries, Walker and Uncle Cletus fought over the zucchini, and the customers hammered at the door. Jordan grinned.

She really loved this business.

The day proved busy and fun and energizing, and by six that evening, with the door closed behind the last customer, Jordan felt pleasantly exhausted. Rainer arrived just as they locked up.

"Come over to the house," Cletus invited in jovial tones.

Jordan looked at her uncle curiously, wondering why he'd become so friendly all of a sudden. Without comment, she led the way home and offered to make coffee.

In the kitchen she stood and stared at the gleaming white coffeemaker, her emotions in turmoil. She'd made her decision yesterday afternoon, she wouldn't allow her personal feelings to interfere in the best interests of Cornucopia. So her present confusion frustrated her. Why wish for the impossible? She didn't have a hope for a future with Rainer—not while Cornucopia stood between them. Besides, her feelings for him were physical, nothing more. And she'd control physical—or ignore it.

He appeared in the doorway, and she immediately realized her error. Her reaction to this man could neither be controlled nor ignored. "I had to come," he admitted in a low voice. "Did you miss me?"

Jordan drew a deep shaky breath, aware she had two choices. She could be honest and tell him she'd missed him more than life itself. That might win her a kiss. Or she could lie through her teeth and save her pride. Jordan thought fast. A kiss...or pride. The hell with it. You only live once.

"I missed you," she admitted with a self-conscious shrug. "A lot. So what do you suggest we do about it?"

His gaze nearly blistered her. "I've got an idea or two."

He crossed to her side and drew her into his arms. He took his time, staring down at her. Then he slowly lowered his head and covered her mouth with his. Intense searing heat raged through her, and automatically her lips parted beneath the hot demand of his.

She felt the kitchen counter biting into her spine, and as though aware of it, he gripped her around the waist and lifted her onto the counter edge. It put them on a more even level, and she was swift to take advantage of the fact, sinking into his embrace.

Eventually she came up for air. "I don't want you to get the wrong idea," she gasped, struggling to catch her breath. "This has nothing to do with Cornucopia. You understand that?"

"I understand precisely what this has to do with," he growled, and kissed her once again. He cupped her head, holding her still. His mouth wandered across her jaw to her ear, catching the lobe between his teeth.

Jordan moaned. This was physical and that was all, she tried to convince herself, lost in the wonder of his touch. It was a chemical need—man and woman and nature. Just a whole bunch of uncontrollable hormones shaken to a fizz in a cauldron of emotional soda water. End of story.

So why did that knowledge hurt so much? Why did she yearn for something more? And why, for the first time, did she wish Cornucopia would go away and never be heard from again?

"Your uncle," he muttered, dragging in a breath. "Your uncle's calling. I think he wants his coffee."

She groaned. "I want a few things myself."

"What?"

What was she saying? "I—I mean, fine. I'll get it. How do you take yours?"

He buried his face against her neck. "With sugar. Lots and lots of sugar."

She dragged herself free of his arms and slid off the counter, looking around in bewilderment. "Cups. We need cups. And milk and sugar." She glanced at him, clearing her throat. "Sugar's bad for your health, you know."

He gave an exaggerated leer. "Tell that to my sweet tooth."

Fortunately Rainer took pity on her and helped set a tray, then carried it through to the living room. Jordan sat down next to her uncle and poured the older man a cup of coffee.

Cletus took the cup, shooting her a sharp look. "What took you?" he asked in a querulous tone, his former affability gone.

"We were discussing the hazards of too much sugar in the diet," Jordan prevaricated brazenly.

"You mean the benefits," Rainer murmured.

Before she could argue, her uncle said, "I presume you came for a reason, Thorsen. Why don't we get down to it? You still trying to wrestle Cornucopia away from us, or have you realized the futility of the notion?"

Rainer's eyebrows shot up. "Futile is it?" He turned to Jordan. "Is that what you've decided after all this time?"

She couldn't prevent a smile. "Once I saw the Thorsen markets, yes." She knew her sudden confidence surprised him, and she used that surprise to hammer home her point.

"You can't take the north end, Rainer. Your brand of store won't fly here. The customers want something different, something only we can provide."

She leaned forward, eager to impress him with her views. "Cornucopia isn't a recipe that can be duplicated. It's unique. It's one of a kind. And it's as different from Thorsen's as night from day."

"Phew! That's quite a speech." He sat back in his chair, lost in thought. "Okay," he said after several minutes of tense silence. "You've convinced me."

Jordan stared at him in amazement. "Really?"

"Really." He stood up, shoving his hands into his pockets. "You're saying Thorsen's needs to change in order to successfully enter the north-end market. I accept that." He nodded. "I do. So...I adapt. I learn what's necessary in order to succeed."

This was not going the way she'd intended. She didn't want him to *adapt;* she wanted him to *quit.* "And who's going to teach you?" she scoffed.

"Exactly. Who?" Cletus echoed.

His eyes gleamed with mischief. "You can."

Jordan gazed at him, stunned. *What* had he said?

"You can," he repeated, as though she'd spoken aloud. "You have the knowledge I need. So, teach me. Take me on for a week. Show me the ropes." He grinned at her, as though he'd offered the perfect solution.

"Ha! Not in a month of Sundays," she said, amused despite herself. "Not in a million years. Not even for a million bucks."

"Well, I can't go as high as a million, but how about a hundred dollars?" Rainer offered.

"Ha and double ha!"

"Two hundred," he wheedled.

"I laugh in your face."

"Five."

"Forget—"

"One thousand and you've got a deal," Cletus said out of the blue.

Jordan and Rainer spun around and stared at him.

"Done!" Thorsen cried triumphantly. "I work for you for one week and—"

"And you pay *us* a thousand dollars," Jordan said in a dry voice. "I wish all our employees were so reasonable."

He looked at her as though just realizing what he'd done. His reluctant smile held a hint of irony. "Okay, so you got me now. But I'll have you in the end." He crossed to Cletus and held out a hand. "I'll report for work first thing Monday morning."

"This is ridiculous—" she began.

Rainer cut her off. "On the contrary. It's perfect. We'll work together and by the end of the week, I'm sure we'll have this whole problem resolved." He held up his hands, silencing any further protests. "Argue while you walk me out to my car," he suggested.

"Fine." She turned and glared at her uncle. "I'll speak to *you* when I finish with *him*." With that she strode from the room.

Rainer caught up with her by the front door. "Don't be too hard on your uncle. It's obvious he wants to be reasonable and work out a deal with us."

She didn't reply, preferring to discuss things far from curious ears. She yanked open the door and stepped outside, tripping over Scratch. She nudged the huge marmalade cat to one side. "Well, don't count on Uncle Cletus being reasonable any time in the near future. He's up to something, and I can guarantee it's not a deal with you Thorsens."

He cocked his head. "This is difficult for you. I understand that." His voice hardened a touch. "But I'm not paying to work for you because I seriously believe there's anything special about the north end."

Jordan blinked in surprise. "But—"

"I'm paying to work with you in the hopes of reaching an equitable solution," he explained.

She sighed. "Look, this is absurd. It won't settle anything, so why don't we just scrap the whole crazy idea?"

He didn't respond, merely folded his arms across his chest in silent refusal.

She tried again. "We settled our…disagreement over the bananas. I'm sure we can work something out here." Her words held a desperate edge. "Let's flip another coin. If I win, we forget about you working here. I'll tell Uncle Cletus you've changed your mind."

He shook his head. "I already have what I want. I don't need to flip a coin for it."

"Yes, you do," she insisted angrily. "Uncle Cletus doesn't run that store. I do. If you force this on me, I'll make sure you regret it. You won't learn one damn thing about the north end or Cornucopia or anything else. The only thing you'll see all week is the inside of the trash Dumpster, because that's where I'll have you working."

He thought about it. "What do I get if I win the toss?"

"What do you want?"

"You mean what do I want in addition to working at Cornucopia?" His grin was slow and suggestive, and told her all too clearly what else he wanted.

She swallowed. "Yes." The word escaped her all by itself.

He lowered his voice to a whisper, the sound dark and rich and enticing. "Yes, I can have what I want? Or yes, what is it I want?"

"Yes—" She had to get a grip! "Yes, the second one."

Rainer chuckled. "Coward. Okay. If I win the toss I want...cooperation."

"That's it?" she asked, vastly relieved. "I can cooperate. I'm sure I can. If I have to."

His eyes narrowed. "With me by your side, count on it."

Time to get down to business. She smiled. Time to win. "Heads or tails?"

"I'll take tails again." He grabbed her hand as she reached into her right pocket. "Only this time we'll use *my* coin," he asserted, giving her a bland smile.

She tried her innocent look. "Please. Allow me."

"No way, my sweet. The jig is up. Nick let me in on your little scam. No double-headed nickels. This time we'll have an honest toss."

Remembered guilt made her squirm. "Or no toss at all?" she suggested with as much panache as she could manage.

He shrugged indifferently. "You're the one who wants me out of Cornucopia. At least this way you've got a fifty-fifty chance. It's better than my chances were with the bananas."

Jordan had the grace to look ashamed. She was lucky he'd let her banana scam slip by with so little...discussion. She should be grateful. Besides, what choice did she have? "Okay. Flip it."

He did so, sending a quarter spinning high in the air. He caught the coin with ease and slapped it on the back of his hand. "Tails," he announced. With a quick flick of his wrist, he palmed the quarter and stuck it in his pocket.

"Hey! What's the big idea? I didn't see which it was." She stared at him in resentment. "That's unfair."

"So sue me." He tucked a hand around the base of her neck and drew her closer. "And consider us square over the bananas."

"Consider *me* ticked off." She flattened her hands against his chest and pushed. Not that it helped. He held her with ease. "Those were my bananas to begin with. Any method I chose to get them back was legitimate. And if you think I'm going to cooperate—"

He lowered his head. "You'll be amazed by the things we eventually cooperate on." And he sealed his words with a kiss.

SNEAKY DEVIL, Jordan thought some time later as she headed back to the house. She raised her fingers to her lips, feeling the warmth that still lingered there. Two could play at that game. She drew herself up short. So, they were back to playing games. If she didn't watch it, she'd find herself benched for the duration. When would she realize that the Thorsens were serious, that this wasn't a game at all?

"Uncle Cletus?" she called, determined to have it out with him.

"In the kitchen," he answered. "You hungry?"

Definitely, though for something far different than food. Not that she could admit as much to her uncle. He'd never understand her defection to the enemy camp. Which is how he'd look at her hormonal interest in Rainer.

She opened the silverware drawer and collected utensils and crossed to set the table. "Are you going to explain, or do I have to dig it out of you?"

"What's to explain?" Uncle Cletus asked a tad too blithely.

She spun to face him. "How could you let him trick you like that? If he comes to work for us, he'll learn all our secrets and put us out of business. Our plans will go right down the tubes."

"Nonsense," he scoffed. "He won't learn a thing."

That took her aback. "How can you be so sure?"

Her uncle smiled a tiny triumphant smile. "Because he doesn't want to *learn* how we do things. He wants to *change* how we do things."

His reasoning gave her pause. "Do you think so?"

"I do. Besides, this way we can keep an eye on him, *and* rake in a thousand bucks to boot." He waved a wooden spoon in her direction. "Just you remember, it's not the train you see that runs you over. It's the train you don't see."

She struggled to hide her exasperation. "That's just great, Uncle Cletus. But when you're tied to the railroad tracks, you're going to get squashed whether you see the train coming or not."

RAINER SHOWED UP Monday morning at Constantine's Wholesale Market. He strode across the loading area to where Jordan and Terry stood talking. "Reporting for work," he announced in a voice loud enough to carry down the full length of the dock.

The salesman glanced from one to the other with obvious interest.

"Take a hike," she said out of the corner of her mouth, refusing to look at Rainer.

"How can I help?" he asked, offering them both a friendly grin.

"By leaving." She didn't bother with subtlety this time. "Go away. Don't bother me. Vamoose. Arrivederci and adios."

"You're trying to tell me something, right?" His brows drew together. "You don't want my help?"

She faced him directly, her hands on her hips. "I've been doing this for a lot of years without any help from you. I intend to continue doing this for a lot more years, again without your help. Our agreement is for you to work at Cornucopia, not here.''

"Wrong." He folded his arms across his chest in a now familiar gesture. "Our agreement is for me to work with you. You're here, therefore I'm here."

"As my *employee*, I, your *employer*, instruct you to leave."

His eyes gleamed with amusement. "Dare I mention the word 'cooperation'?"

"No, you dare not."

"Cooperation."

"So sue me!" she said, throwing his own words back in his face. She glared at Terry. "What are you laughing at? You want to sell me some lettuce, or does Nick have to stock up on rabbits?"

Terry's face was wiped clean of its smile. "Lettuce. Coming right up." He led the way to the refrigerated "wet room," Jordan and Rainer in close pursuit. He pointed to the floor-to-ceiling pallet loads of iced-down lettuce, green onions and radishes. "What's your pleasure?"

"Iceberg, bib, red, green and—" she glanced down at her clipboard and checked her list "—butter lettuce. Oh, and throw in a crate of radishes."

"You got it." Terry pushed his cart through the puddles of water to the end of the room and began to load up.

Jordan looked at Rainer and sighed. "It isn't necessary for you to follow me around like this. It won't teach you anything new about Cornucopia."

"On the contrary," he countered. "There's plenty it will teach me. Since the north end is so unique in your opinion, the choices you make will give me insight into your customers. I can also judge potential sales by the size of your order."

Terry walked by, his cart loaded down. He whistled tune-lessly, acting as though he were blind and deaf to their little skirmish.

She waited until he'd pushed through the heavy plastic strips that served as an insulated door before resuming their discussion. "It's embarrassing, having you trail along behind me. People will talk."

She could see her concern cut no ice with him. "Tough. I'm here. I'm staying. And you're cooperating. Understand?"

"Do I have a choice?"

"None."

Jordan lifted her chin. "Then I understand." She stalked to the door and shoved her way through the plastic strips, silently fuming.

The nerve of the man. No way could she get through a full week with his watching her every move. And no way could she get through a full week of all the stares and not-so-subtle comments flying back and forth along the dock. It wouldn't take long before someone tackled her about them. She wondered who would be first.

She didn't have long to wait. Andrea cornered her near a pallet of green bananas. "When are you gassing these greenies?" Jordan asked, attempting to play for time. "I need some yellows."

"Tomorrow, and stalling won't work. What is going on?" Andrea demanded in an undertone. "You can't believe the rumors I've been hearing."

"Sure I can." Jordan started ticking off the items on her fingers. "One. Rainer's after Cornucopia—which you knew. Two. He's spying on us—which you also knew. Three. He thinks he can get the store through me." She grinned. "I hope you know better than that."

"Four. They say you're sleeping with him. I hope *you* know better than *that*." At Jordan's shocked expression, Andrea hastened to add, "No, I don't believe the rumor's true. No, don't waste your breath denying it. And no, I wouldn't take it lightly, if I were you."

Jordan closed her eyes. "Damn."

"Don't worry." Andrea smiled with satisfaction. "I nipped possibility number four right in the bud."

"Is the guilty party still walking?"

"Just. And what walking he does is with a limp." She eyed Jordan keenly. "So what's going on? If you haven't been fool enough to fall for the Thorsen charm like I did, what are you doing here with Rainer?"

"I don't have any choice," Jordan admitted, then explained the situation with Uncle Cletus in a few terse sentences. "My back was up against the wall."

Andrea groaned. "It's suicide, pure and simple. You might as well hand him the market—lock, stock and banana peels. He's too powerful. Fighting Rainer, or any of the Thorsens for that matter, is like trying to hold back the tide."

She was right, Jordan acknowledged. He *was* powerful. And like the tide, he swept away all her good intentions. Despite herself, she remembered the potency of his kisses, the strength of his touch, and the intensity of the passion he could so easily arouse. She chewed her lip distractedly. What on earth would she do?

Rainer's approach was as silent as it was unnerving. "Are you through buying?" He glanced at Andrea, his eyes alert and assessing. "I'm not interrupting something, am I?"

"No, not at all," Andrea said, and turned away.

Jordan grimaced, realizing that despite her friend's intense dislike for the Thorsens, she couldn't afford to offend them. Not without incensing her father. Looked like she and

Andrea were both neatly caught, each in her own particular trap.

"I want to check out Nick's specialty room before we leave," Jordan informed Rainer. "Where's Terry?"

"Writing up your order and loading the truck. I told him I'd cart out anything else you need. You want to settle up with the cashier in the meantime?"

She shot him an angry glance. High-handed Viking! Did he think after ten years in the business, she couldn't take care of her own needs? "There's nothing to settle," she informed him tightly. "We have a line of credit."

His eyebrows shot up and then his expression turned bland. "Lucky you."

Without a word she walked away. This would have to stop, she determined. He knew entirely too much about their business. As soon as they got back to Cornucopia, a few ground rules would be laid down—laid down like a steamroller over pavement.

JORDAN PULLED into the driveway of Cornucopia and drove around to the side, careful as she backed the truck up to the loading dock. She'd been acutely aware of the sporty red convertible following her all the way to the store. By the time she slammed out of the truck, her temper flashed past the boiling point.

"Not here," he said, accurately reading her expression. He grabbed her arm, hustling her around the back of the store toward the house.

"Take your hands off me!" she demanded, fighting vainly against his hold.

He stopped in his tracks. "Your choice. Inside and private, or out here and public."

"In."

"Key."

She shoved her hand into her pocket and yanked out the house key, slapping it into his palm. Lord, he looked intimidating. But she refused to be intimidated. Not her. No way. Not intimidated in the least.

"This isn't going to work," she announced the second they were through the door.

"Oh, yes, it is." He stared down at her from his great height, his eyes cold and stormy, his face set in lines of determination. "We're going to thrash this out here and now."

"That should be my line," she griped.

Not a hint of amusement lit his gaze. "By all means. Begin."

"Fine." She started pacing. "This is how it is. You've conned my uncle into allowing you to work at Cornucopia and learn all our secrets, but you're not conning me."

"I didn't realize I'd tried to con you."

She paused, color warming her cheeks. "You know what I'm talking about. You've...you've tried to bamboozle me."

"I've kissed you."

"Exactly." Her pacing resumed. "Bamboozled me with your kisses. I'm not complaining about that," she hastened to add. "I'm willing to let it go."

"Generous of you."

She ignored his comment. "I'm also willing to put up with you at the store for the week as agreed," she continued doggedly. "But I won't have you buying with me in the mornings. That isn't part of the deal."

"I say it is." He studied her closely for a moment, then asked, "What did she say? And don't pretend you don't know what I'm talking about. Andrea Constantine—what did she say to you? Though I think I can guess."

"Feel free. But she hasn't said anything that isn't being bandied about the docks already."

A glimmer of amusement touched his features. "Ah. Now I understand. You and me. Me and you. The hint of romance. The suggestion of an affair."

"So you see why I don't want you coming with me anymore." She gazed up at him hopefully.

"I do."

Jordan grinned. "Then it's settled."

"It is not."

Her grin vanished. "What?"

He dropped his hands onto her shoulders. "I sympathize with your feelings, and I'm sorry today proved so uncomfortable. But the damage has been done, and I have a job to do."

"Your job is more important than my reputation?"

"I am not damaging your reputation," he stated coldly. "We are not sleeping together. Yet. And even if we were, it's no one's business but our own."

Yet. What did he mean, *yet?* She flushed. Who was she kidding? She knew full well what he meant. The thought sent chills racing through her. She wanted him, she admitted. She'd tried to convince herself it was simple lust. But it wasn't simple, nor lust alone. She cared about this man— honestly, sincerely cared.

"Please, Rainer," she whispered.

He shook his head. "If you'd like, I'll make it clear to Nick that I'm interested in purchasing Cornucopia. He can make sure the rumors are stopped. But I'm coming with you in the mornings, Jordan, and that's all there is to it. If you can't handle it, have your uncle buy this week and I'll go with him."

"You know that's impossible! He couldn't... He's not..."

"Then he doesn't belong in the business and you should urge him to give serious consideration to our offer. I'm amazed that you've managed so long on your own. When do you have time for yourself?''

''It's my life!'' she shot at him. ''Stop trying to tell me how to live it.''

''You don't have a life,'' he shot back. ''You have a job.''

''Which I can do without any advice from you. I don't need you!''

''Yes you do.'' He tugged her closer, his grip on her shoulders tightening. ''And while we have the privacy to discuss it, I expect your full cooperation this week, as promised.''

''You'll get it.''

''I know I will.'' He gave her a gentle shake. ''Jordan, don't fight me. You won't win—''

''Stop telling me that!''

''Stop fighting!'' His hands slid from her shoulders to her arms and then around her. ''Stop fighting,'' he whispered the words again. He drew her close, enfolding her in his embrace. His lips brushed hers, teasing, driving her wild with need.

She moaned softly. ''You'll take everything if I don't fight you. I'll have nothing left. I can't give it all up.''

He kissed her, his touch infinitely tender. ''Do you think I only take? You don't know me very well, my love. But you will.''

Jordan closed her eyes. She didn't dare look at him, didn't dare see the expression in those sea-washed eyes. If she did, she knew she'd be lost for all time.

He kissed her. Again. And finally, unable to resist, she gave in.

CHAPTER SEVEN

NOT LONG AFTERWARD, they returned to the market. Jordan took in the threatened chaos, grateful for the work still remaining. This she knew how to do. This she understood. Cornucopia didn't leave her dizzy and confused. Cornucopia didn't turn her six ways to Sunday.

Why did Rainer? She didn't understand her emotional state. It must be a hormonal imbalance. Even lust she could accept better than the alternative. She closed her eyes. It wasn't love. It couldn't be. She didn't have the time or the experience to love someone like Rainer.

She glanced at him furtively. He looked her way just then and she froze, praying her apprehension didn't show. She'd gotten in too deep. The knowledge crystallized in her mind, growing, expanding, filling her with dread. She forced her gaze away from his, staring blindly at a haphazard stack of corn crates. Time to pull back and regroup. Fast. Time to find a way out.

Uncle Cletus had made the biggest mistake of their lives when he invited this man to work with them. It was like setting the cat loose among the pigeons. And from the expression on Rainer's face, he found pigeon pie mighty tasty.

"Where do we start?" he asked pragmatically enough.

Relieved, she drew a deep breath and looked around. "Let's see . . . I have Andy and Leroy sorting and displaying the roots. Uncle Cletus always takes care of the salad fixings. And Walker handles the remaining vegetables. Michelle sets up the cash register. That leaves you to organize..."

"The rest?"

She glanced up at him with suspicion. Not a flicker of irony, or anything else for that matter, showed in his expression. "It's all yours," she agreed.

"And you'll be doing...?"

"Prices, signs and troubleshooting." She couldn't help smiling. "Lots of troubleshooting."

If she'd expected Rainer to question every move she made, she learned differently in short order. True, he kept close watch of her activities. But if he formed any opinions as a result, he didn't voice them. He also worked harder than anyone Jordan had ever seen, accomplishing more in five minutes than she could in thirty. By the time the store opened at nine, they'd completed every last task.

Jordan shook her head in amazement. "I never thought it possible," she muttered.

"That's because you never had me at your side." His eyes contained a warm almost protective gleam. "See what a little help will do?"

She stirred uneasily. "Thanks. I appreciate it."

Only she didn't, and he knew it.

"So I see." He selected a grape from the display he'd arranged and popped it into his mouth. "Don't let the improved routine bother you, love. I'm in the business, remember? I know what I'm doing. And I can put out strawberries with the best of them. You should be upset if it *hadn't* gone well."

Jordan laughed, relaxing a little. "I'm being silly. I've always wanted everything done when we opened the front doors." She gestured to encompass the picture-perfect shop. "Here I get my wish, and I'm still not happy."

"Because I gave it to you."

She caught her lip in her teeth, wishing she could deny his statement but unable to. How could she, when it held a certain validity? She offered him a wry smile. "Now I feel like a heel. I'm being defensive, aren't I?"

"Territorial would be more accurate." He moved nearer, his voice dropping a notch. "I know all about territorial." He lowered his head, his lips close to her ear, his warm breath stirring the curls at her temple. "I take what I want and I hold what I have. No one takes what's mine. Is that what you're feeling?"

"Yes. I'm also hearing warning bells," she murmured with a shiver.

"Listen to them." He straightened. "In the meantime, show me some of the things that make Cornucopia so unique."

I take what I want—he wanted Cornucopia—*and I hold what I have.* He'd never let go once he had her store. *No one takes what's mine.* Did he already consider the market his? The cat was getting ever closer to the pigeons. Heaven help her tail feathers.

"Jordan?"

She struggled to switch gears. "What?"

"You were going to show me what makes Cornucopia unique."

"Unique...unique..." She looked around the store with a blank stare.

"How about the interesting wall coverings."

She bristled at the implied criticism. Uncle Cletus was right. He did want to change things. Well, let him try—and let him fail. "What about them?"

He crossed the room and studied the artwork she'd hung there. Picture after childish picture showed different arrangements of fruits and vegetables. An occasional rendition of Uncle Cletus or Walker or herself were among the colorful collage.

"It's cute, but not very professional."

"Says you." Jordan lifted her chin. "These pictures are done by my customers' children. They use that back table I have set up and draw while their parents shop."

He glanced at the table she indicated, his expression doubtful. It took up one corner of the market. Against the wall, behind the table, stood a low shelf stuffed full of books. On the table were markers, crayons and paper, scraps of material, scissors and glue.

"I've been meaning to ask you about that," he said. "If you put produce counters in that corner instead, you could increase sales by, oh..."

"Ten percent or more," she said, wondering if her voice sounded as arid to him as it did to her.

"Don't get me wrong," he hastened to say. "It's nice and everything. But you're running a business. Having a kids area and running tabs on special customers—Seth, for instance—and then throwing their bills away... It's not..."

"Not professional?" She offered him a bland smile, darned if she'd explain her reasoning. Seth was a personal project and her most loyal customer. As for the kids corner... well, Rainer'd chosen to work for Cornucopia for a week. Let him work and learn. "You're right. It's probably a mistake." She looked around. "What else are we doing wrong?"

He laughed, holding up his hands. "Okay, okay. I surrender. I'll watch and listen, and draw my own conclusions. At the end of the week, we'll discuss your... uniqueness again."

"Good plan." And this time he couldn't mistake her dry tone.

THE WEEK FLEW BY. Jordan became accustomed to having Rainer shop with her at the wholesale market. She didn't know what he said to Nick, but it stopped all open speculation cold. If there was any private speculation going on, not a whisper of it reached her.

At Cornucopia things progressed just as smoothly. His help proved invaluable, and to her disgust and inner fury, she found herself counting on it more and more. He knew so much about the business and dealt so well with people. In addition, he was big and strong and . . .

Even Uncle Cletus seemed to take an unexpected liking to him, happily discussing philosophy, religion and economics, as well as its effect on produce. Not by a flicker of an eyelash did Rainer show amusement or disdain. He listened seriously and commented seriously. It made her all the more wary.

She couldn't allow herself to forget his true purpose. The man was helping them for a reason. And it wasn't altruism.

Brooding about it, Jordan watched him while he chatted with Marie Langstrom, a pretty redhead and a regular customer. A vague jealousy stirred within her, and she frowned, impatient with herself. She knew full well the woman possessed a delightful husband and a brood of children. The knowledge didn't seem to help one lick.

I take what I want and I hold what I have.

His words echoed again through her mind. That was precisely how she felt this very minute. She wished she could march up to that flirty redhead and toss her right out of the store. She cringed. Territorial feelings about Cornucopia she could understand. But about Rainer? She shook her head. No way. This meant trouble. Big trouble.

She scrambled to assess the amount of damage and figure a way to contain it before it grew worse. What were her angles? What was her out? Her eyes widened. She really had turned into a spiral staircase.

"Jordan?" A shy voice said at her elbow.

Startled, she whipped around and looked into the smiling face of Marie's eight-year-old daughter. "Casey, I didn't see you there!"

"I found something to draw, but I don't know what it is."

"Let's find out," Jordan suggested. "Is it a fruit, or a vegetable?"

The girl thought for a moment. "It's brown," she said decisively.

"Brown." Jordan grinned. "Brown works. Why don't you show it to me?" She followed Casey back to the kids counter, where Casey and her brother had spread open a number of books.

"This one." Casey pointed to a picture.

"It's a fruit called a kiwi. That ugly brown outside hides a delicious green inside. Come on, I'll show you."

Having gained both children's interest, she went over to the fruit counter and selected a ripe kiwifruit. She took the knife used to trim lettuce and sliced the egg-sized fruit into four sections.

"They're very sweet," Jordan explained, "and you can even eat the little black seeds." She peeled back the skin and nibbled at the bright green fruit. "Have a taste."

Exchanging hesitant glances, the children each took a section and followed Jordan's example. Their uncertainty changed to astonished delight, and they ran to their mother, begging her to buy some kiwifruit. She could hear Marie's laughing agreement.

Rainer looked at her from across the store. Did she see comprehension dawning in his eyes? If he thought she kept the children's corner for this reason alone, he'd find himself sadly mistaken. She loved teaching the children about the different produce the market carried. She also liked her customers and their families to feel comfortable in her store—as relaxed here as they were at home.

"I always shop at Cornucopia," she could hear Marie telling Rainer. "I'd never go anywhere else."

"Why is that?"

"Because I can take my time and not worry about the children getting into trouble," came the immediate response. "And they've learned so much! Before they were such picky eaters. Now, thanks to Jordan, their diet is healthier and more varied than mine."

Jordan smiled in satisfaction. That described Cornucopia perfectly. It also explained why Thorsen's markets wouldn't succeed in drawing off her customer base. Uncle Cletus's idea wasn't so foolish, after all, she realized, and felt the first stirring of hope. Maybe Rainer would change his mind, and he and the rest of the Thorsens would leave Cornucopia alone. There was room for both of them in the north end, if he went far enough north—like to Alaska.

SATURDAY DAWNED bright and clear and beautiful, and Jordan headed across the Ballard Bridge on the way to the wholesale market. A faint blush of purplish blue lit the still waters of the canal. From her position in the cab of her truck, she could see a family of ducks swimming around a solitary fishing boat berthed at Fisherman's Terminal.

She felt a certain sadness that today represented Rainer's last at Cornucopia. Still, she couldn't contain her curiosity about his intentions. Had he reached any conclusions? More importantly, had he given up? She hoped so, even though part of her would regret his departure.

This business tended to be a lonely one. Until his advent into her life, she'd never been conscious of that. His company this past week brought it home to her. He'd been a partner, and she found she liked having a partner.

She pulled into Constantine's, surprised when she didn't immediately spot Rainer's red convertible. She waited in the truck for a while, expecting him to show at any moment. Fifteen minutes later, she gave up. Time waited for no man—nor did work. She climbed out of the cab and clambered onto the docks. Rainer could catch up later.

Jordan trudged alongside Terry and placed her order, annoyed at the sensation of loss that nagged at her.

"The big guy bail out on you?" Terry asked with a guilty surreptitious look around.

"Don't worry. Nick's nowhere to be seen," she informed him. "And yes, it appears you're safe from Thorsen, as well."

"Really?" The salesman brightened. "So what gives? You and him an item, or what?"

"Did I just declare open hunting season or something?" she muttered. "No, you can safely announce the length of the dock that Rainer and I are not an item."

"Rainer, huh?" was all he said. Which was enough.

Terry's "big guy" didn't show up at the wholesale market at all that morning. Nor was he waiting at Cornucopia. As a result, setup proved a disaster. Nothing went right. Andy and Leroy nearly came to blows, as did Uncle Cletus and Walker. Michelle couldn't have found the puddles to mop if she'd been drowning in them. And Jordan...Jordan was not happy.

Two minutes before opening, she stood in front of her uncle, her hands on her hips. "You *have* to put out the pickling cukes. That's why we bought them. It's also why we bought the dill." She pointed at the huge stalks of the lacy herb sitting in a bucket of water. "Dill plus pickling cucumbers equals pickles. Get it? Our customers can't pickle without pickling supplies." She'd begun to feel like Peter Piper.

Cletus cradled the bulky carton of cucumbers in his arms. "What about what the cukes want?"

She balled her hands into fists and spoke through gritted teeth. "The cukes live to be pickled. They want it with every fiber of their runted gnarly little bodies."

Her uncle's grip tightened on the box. "If Rainer were here, he'd understand."

"Well, he's not, I am, and you're out of luck," she snarled. "Now hand 'em over."

A deep voice intruded on their conversation. "Problem?"

Jordan and Cletus turned. Cletus beamed at Rainer. She scowled.

"Rainer, my boy. Just the one I wished to see." He shot his niece a reproachful look. "It's about these cukes...."

Rainer touched her arm. "It's past nine and customers are waiting. Why don't you open up," he suggested. "I'll take care of this."

Barely able to contain her fury, she stomped to the door and swung it open. "I hope you don't want pickles," she snapped at the first little old lady in line. "Because you're not likely to get any."

"No, no," the woman assured her in a timid voice. "I don't want pickles. In fact, I don't think I want anything at all."

Before the poor old soul could scurry away, Jordan ushered her into the store, feeling lower than a snake's belly. "Sure you do," she soothed. "Have a spaghetti squash. On the house."

The woman hesitated. "Well...I suppose I could choke one down."

"And I'd be delighted to help you—" Her arm was grasped from behind and before she could draw breath, Rainer hustled her away from the front door. "Hey, what—"

"Back," he said.

"Forget it!"

"Public."

Jordan sighed, giving up. "Lunchroom."

"Now that's truly *unique*," he bit out, the instant they hit the lunchroom. "Of all the *unique* things I've seen in my life, that one tops them all."

Jordan felt tears start. "I know. I know. I'm sorry. I'm a total louse. I can't believe I did that. My only excuse is that it's been a rotten morning." She shoved a tumble of dark curls back from her face. "Nothing around here is done, everyone is fighting, and I've been reduced to yelling at the customers." Her lower lip inched out. "And it's all your fault."

"*My* fault? How the hell do you figure?"

"Because you weren't here . . ." She closed her eyes and groaned, unable to believe what she'd just said.

She opened her eyes to his kiss. It was gentle and loving and warmed her from top to bottom. He held her lightly, his touch one of comfort instead of passion, and gratitude filled her at his insight. She needed his comfort right now.

Her hands crept up his chest, clinging to the hard muscles of his shoulders. Never before had she felt so vulnerable, never before had she taken such delight in his strength. His lips moved slowly over hers and the urge to fight faded away. She settled deeper into his protective embrace.

"Jordan, someone might walk in," he murmured, fitting her hips more firmly into the cradle of his.

Her breath caught in her throat at the intimate contact. "When you hold me like this, I almost don't care." She glanced up, gripped by uncertainty. "I guess I shouldn't admit that."

A smile eased his features. "I'm glad you did."

She ran her fingers down the side of his face, her hand striking the tiny gold earring he wore. She pulled back a little, studying it, touching it gently.

"I've always wondered about this," she owned. "Thorsen. Son of Thor. Is that why you have a lightning bolt, because it's one of Thor's symbols?"

"Yes—and more." He hesitated. "It's a reminder."

Her curiosity grew. "Of what?"

He didn't immediately respond. She waited, and at last he said, "Of heritage. Of family. Of what it takes to succeed."

Of all the things that stood between them, in fact. No wonder he'd been reluctant to answer. She grimaced. "I wish I hadn't asked."

"Thor has one, too," he told her. "It's a tiny hammer."

The better to clobber her with? The better to bring down Cornucopia? She refused to think about that. Not now. Not here. Not when she felt so safe and secure within the circle of Rainer's arms. A tiny sigh escaped her. "I think I prefer the lightning bolt," she told him shyly.

If he knew how much the confession cost her, he didn't let on. "I'm glad to hear it." He touched her mouth with a callused fingertip. "I have a favor to ask you."

She shivered in apprehension. "What?"

"Don't look so worried." He smiled, reaching out to tuck a stray curl behind her ear. "I'd like to stay on an extra week. That's what made me late today—arranging for Thor to take over a little longer in case you agree."

She wanted to agree. She wanted to agree more than anything in the world. "Why?" she asked instead. "Why stay on?"

"Several reasons. You must know I haven't learned everything necessary about Cornucopia and the north-end market. We're also no closer to settling our...disagreement over the store's future, and..."

"And?" Her voice held a breathless quality she despised.

"*We* have things left to settle," he confessed gruffly. "Private things."

Jordan lowered her eyes, delighted by his admission. Not that she wanted Rainer to know that. He had enough power over her. Any more wouldn't be good for him. Nor would it be good for her.

"I think I can talk Uncle Cletus into letting you stay on," she agreed offhandedly. "And I'll make it a bargain. You'll only have to pay us five hundred to work this week."

"Gee, thanks."

Her grin was cheeky. "Anytime."

He bent his head and gave her a final lingering kiss. "Ready to face the riots and hysteria?"

"Let me at 'em!" She paused, a sudden thought occurring. "By the way, did you convince Uncle Cletus to put out the pickling cukes?"

"Of course."

"How?" she asked suspiciously.

"Simple," he retorted with a bland smile. "I asked him."

To her amazement everything fell right into place. Though why it would amaze her, she didn't know. Rainer's special brand of charm was guaranteed to work miracles. He could accomplish more with a lifted eyebrow than she could with an hour of exhaustive argument. And he had a knack for keeping everyone pleasant and cheerful—including her.

The day flew by, each moment precious and each moment fleeting. It seemed impossible that she'd managed alone for so long. Not that she'd been entirely alone, she hastened to remind herself. She mustn't forget Uncle Cletus. Thinking of him made her smile. The man was unquestionably a darling, but he knew as much about the business end of things as she knew about... about the political affiliation of cabbage.

A continuous stream of shoppers kept them so busy that Rainer didn't even comment when Jordan slipped a bedraggled looking Seth some free produce. But finally the last customer left. Cleaning up the store and putting away the stock—usually a chore—seemed pleasurable with Rainer there. Within thirty minutes they'd completed the last task. The employees dashed off for their Saturday-evening activities, and Walker and Cletus decided to head back to the house for a quiet game of checkers.

Rainer flipped off the overhead lights, all but one row. Though still light outside, the interior was dim and quiet.

"Do you have time to talk?" he asked, watching as she counted out the change from the till.

"Sure. What would you like to talk about?"

"Cornucopia." She lifted her head in alarm, relieved by his reassuring smile. "Not that," he dismissed. "I mean about the things you do here. The things you do differently than Thorsen's."

"Ah, our uniqueness again. You've been here a whole week and you haven't gotten a handle on it yet?" she dared to tease.

"There're a lot of things I haven't gotten a handle on. But we'll stick with Cornucopia for the time being." He approached the checkout stand where she stood, and edged his hip onto a corner. "I think I understand why you have the children's table. It takes up valuable selling space, and it probably wouldn't work in all of our stores. But here—" he shrugged "—it fits. It feels right."

"That's because it is right." She began to record the cheques on the deposit slip. "What else bothers you?"

"I won't mention your various charity cases, like that Seth character."

Her lips tightened. "I appreciate your restraint."

"But I do question the free samples you give out. I know in theory customers supposedly buy more if they try it first. But in actuality, it costs you about what you make in profits."

Jordan chuckled. "Let's just say it's my way of expanding our customers' horizons a little. Mrs. Johnson wouldn't buy a mango if it sat up and begged. It's too exotic. But she gets an illicit thrill sneaking a sample here."

He seemed to accept her explanation. "And the organic produce? That's a double loser. It spoils fast, and it has a limited customer base."

"Carry the five, and six is eleven." She jotted down the number and stuck the deposit slip into the bank bag before continuing, "There you're way off. I have a select clientele who only buy organically grown produce. One or two are somewhat chi-chi-pooh-pooh. But most are very environmentally concerned." She looked up at him and grinned. "That 'loser,' as you call it, constitutes thirty percent of my business at a nice comfortable profit."

He looked surprised. "You're serious."

"Yes, I'm serious." She could see she'd intrigued him.

"If they like that, have you thought about carrying cheese and tofu?" He scrutinized the store. "Over there." He pointed toward the "organic" section of the market. "Against that wall. You'd have to move those pictures, but you could put in a big refrigerated case with a variety of specialty cheeses. Tofu, bean curd, sprouts, that sort of thing."

"Move my family pictures?" She dismissed the idea without further consideration. "Forget it."

"Why?"

"Because those pictures represent the history of this store. Some of them have hung there for so long they've probably grown roots. I wouldn't move them for all the bananas in Costa Rica."

Rainer walked over to examine the pictures, and Jordan followed. "I've never really looked at them before," he said, studying each one with interest. He pointed to the first. "Is this your grandfather?"

"Yes, that's Grandpa Joe," she said proudly. She indicated the storefront in the photograph, and the sign that hung over her grandfather's head. "Back then we were called Roberts' Food and Froth."

"Froth?"

She chuckled. "As in soft drinks. When Dad and Uncle Cletus took over, they changed the name to Cornucopia and decided to specialize in just produce and dairy products."

"What happened to the dairy part?"

Jordan shrugged. "We let it go after Dad died. Actually, I've been tempted to get back into it. I like your suggestion about the cheeses, but they just can't go here." She touched another picture. "That's my mother right after I was born. It's the only photo with all the Roberts."

Rainer put a hand on her shoulder, squeezing gently as though in sympathy for all she'd lost. She leaned back against him, the heat from his body warming her, chasing away the chill. Awareness crept over her and she struggled to breathe normally, to speak as though she wasn't conscious of every movement he made, every sound he uttered and every breath he took.

"This last picture is of Uncle Cletus and me. If you check carefully, you can see Walker peering through the front store window. He didn't want to be left out, poor guy."

Obediently Rainer leaned closer to get a better look. "Why didn't he join you and Cletus outside?"

"Uncle Cletus wouldn't let him. He said Walker wasn't officially family." She wrinkled her nose. "Personally I didn't agree. When you have so few in your family, you're always on the lookout for more members."

"And the few you have become very important to you," he added in complete understanding.

"Yes," she whispered. "Especially when they've loved you and cared for you and raised you. Especially when they've... *he* has never asked anything, but instead given everything."

"And Cornucopia?"

"It's also family, though in a different way." Filled with an urge to explain, she gazed up at him. "It's my connection to the past. It's all I have left of my parents, of my heritage. You wear an earring as a reminder. Yet all you have to do is go home, and you have it all—your parents, your brother and sister, more aunts and uncles and cousins than a raisin has wrinkles. I... I have Uncle Cletus... and Cornucopia."

"I understand what you're saying, but..." He hesitated, choosing his words with care. "Cornucopia is no substitute for family. Nor is it a substitute for a social life."

She turned away from him, wrapping her arms around herself. How could she explain the loyalty she owed her parents' memory? "Your brother thinks I should take the money and run. But where would I run to? To Arizona and Uncle Cletus's chicken ranch?" She gave an ironic laugh. "This is all I have. Cornucopia *is* family, no matter what you say. I'll never abandon it. And despite his talk about chicken ranches, neither will Uncle Cletus."

"Jordan—"

She turned around, the words exploding from her. "Give it up, Rainer. Leave us alone. Leave *me* alone. Go back to your life, and allow us to return to ours. You don't need Cornucopia. You have dozens of other markets."

A muscle worked in his jaw. "That's not my decision to make. I wish it were, but I have other considerations."

"What else is there to consider? You understand the importance of family. I know you do. Don't take mine away!"

"I don't want to!" He shut his eyes, taking a deep breath. "I can't resolve this based solely on my own preferences."

"Why not?"

He gripped her shoulders, speaking earnestly. "Listen to me, Jordan. There are a lot of people who depend on me and my decisions. No store in the Thorsen chain stands alone. Each is a vital link in the corporation. The family as a whole is dependent on the chain as a whole. I have a responsibility to them and to their employees. They all have a stake in our business."

"You don't need us," she pleaded. "You can go around us."

He shook his head. "Not successfully. Not the way things are now. Honey, Cornucopia stands in a prime location between a juncture of several communities. We could go around you, go farther north, but it would severely hurt our ability to expand. It's essential we acquire Cornucopia. And I can't arbitrarily decide not to take you on, not for personal reasons."

"So what are you going to do?" She could barely get the words out.

"I'm going to work here another week. I'm going to talk some more to Cletus. And then we're all going to sit down and see if we can't reach an amicable solution."

Jordan crossed her arms. "I don't see what it could be. There's nothing we can even compromise over. One of us wins. And one of us loses."

Rainer cocked an eyebrow. "This from the woman who has more angles than a spiral staircase?"

Her eyes widened. "Uncle Cletus told you that?"

"I think it was in the nature of a warning." He began to chuckle. Unable to resist, she joined in. He caught her hands in his. "Give it another week and let's see what happens. Then we'll talk again. Between the two of us, we should be able to come up with something."

"All right," she agreed reluctantly. "One more week."

"Good. Now I have another favor to ask you, Valkyrie."

She licked her lips. Lord, this man expected a lot. Sometimes she didn't think he'd be satisfied with less than all sixty-five inches of her, with her heart thrown in on top.

"Huh! Fat chance," she told him, though what she really meant was, *Ask me for the earth and I'll give it to you, along with the sun and the moon and planets, too.*

Not that she'd tell him that.

He smiled down at her, his eyes warm and a dark forest green. "I want you tonight," he said. "May I have you?"

CHAPTER EIGHT

YES, YES, YES! Jordan almost screamed. "You, what?" she said instead.

"I heard that yes." Rainer grinned. "Shall I ignore it, or give you a hard time?"

"Ah . . . the ignore choice."

A teasing gleam sparkled in his eyes. "No way. I want you—you want me. I heard a yes. End of story. Let's go."

She swallowed. "Where?"

His laughter died away, an intent awareness taking its place. "Anywhere," he said, his words taut and urgent. "Name it."

Jordan shook her head, unable to speak, aching for him with a passion so great she practically shook with it. But she couldn't give in to the urge. She shut her eyes, trying to block out the need mirrored so clearly in his face. "Don't, Rainer. We can't." She looked at him again, watching him struggle between desire and common sense.

"Okay," he said at last. "I'll let it go—this time. I have an alternative. It won't be as much fun—" he shrugged "—but we'll be together."

"What is it?"

"Come with me to my father's birthday party tonight."

Of all the things she'd expected him to suggest, this placed last on the list. In fact, it didn't even make her list. "Why? More business discussions?"

His eyes darkened and his voice held a rough edge. "No. Personal reasons. Very personal."

"I can't—"

"Go where?" Cletus called out, and Jordan took a hasty step away from Rainer. Her uncle peered at them from the back doorway, his expression vaguely puzzled. "You two still here? Where are you going?"

Jordan glanced at Rainer. "Nowhere," she said firmly.

"To my father's sixtieth-birthday party." He glared at her. "Why won't you come?"

"It's not that I won't," she hastened to assure him. "I can't. There's this newspaper ad I should finish. I'd like to join you, but—"

"More work?" The gibe stung.

Cletus crossed over to them, glancing from one to the other. "I can do it," he volunteered. "You never go out, Jordan. I'd feel bad if you worked tonight."

"Looks like I'm not the only one who thinks you should have more of a social life," Rainer commented in an aside.

She shot him a disgruntled look, before addressing her uncle. "That's sweet of you, but—"

"No, no. I insist." He beamed. "It's the least I can do."

She wanted to go. She really wanted to go. She also knew there was no way on God's green earth her uncle could handle that ad. Not after his latest escapade with the sign changes. Something of her thoughts must have shown in her face.

"Don't you trust me to do it?" Cletus asked in a pained voice.

What could she tell him? Certainly not the truth. Not with Rainer looking on. "Of course I trust you. And I appreciate the offer, it's just . . ."

The saying "caught between a rock and a hard place" took on special meaning. Jordan sighed, knowing she didn't have a choice. She'd have to let Uncle Cletus do the ad—and she'd have to be certain to check it before it went out.

Satisfied at reaching a workable solution, she gave in gracefully. "Thank you, Uncle Cletus. If you're sure it's not too much trouble...."

"No trouble at all." He grinned happily and hurried off, calling for Walker.

"Well, it seems we're on," she said to Rainer. "Give me a minute to change?"

"I'll give you five," he offered magnanimously.

It took her ten. And it was worth every extra minute to see the look in his eyes as she reentered the store.

"You're beautiful," he declared in his husky voice. "Purple's a great color on you. It makes your eyes all dark and smoky. I'm not sure we should go to my parents', after all. I'd rather be alone with you."

Self-consciously, she touched the full amethyst-colored skirt of her dress and smiled. "I think we'd be safer at your parents'."

"For a few hours...maybe."

Her smile died. That's all they had—a few hours. Just a brief respite before the world came crashing in again. "And then we'll be right back to where we started, fighting over Cornucopia."

"Don't," he said softly. "Not tonight. Forget the store. Forget about Cletus and work and shoulds and shouldn'ts. Let's be selfish and take one night for ourselves. What do you say?"

Jordan gazed up at him, troubled. "Is that possible?"

He touched her shoulder, his hand sliding up the length of her neck to burrow in the loose hair about her shoulders. "We'll make it possible."

"I'd like that," she agreed, the tension draining from her.

It only took a few minutes to drive to the Thorsens. Jordan stepped out of the car and gazed up at the full August moon, the soft white glow reflecting off the dark waters of Puget Sound. In the distance the lights of the ferries twinkled, as they moved back and forth between Pier 52 and Bainbridge Island.

"Nervous?" he asked. "I know your last visit wasn't..."

"A smashing success?"

"I'll be close by all night," he assured her, tucking her hand through the crook of his arm. "No football games with the kids."

She felt a surge of relief. "Is it a formal dinner?"

"Nope. It'll be smorgasbord." He gave the word its Norwegian inflection. "Some people believe the idea originated with the Vikings."

"Of course," she murmured in a dry tone.

"Honest. They'd bring back all these different foods from their raids. Naturally there'd only be a small helping of each, so—voilà."

"French. Meaning 'there it is,'" she said.

"Ah, Valkyrie. You never give in, do you?"

"Never."

He chuckled. "Have you ever had *Kjøttkaker?*" She shook her head. "Good. You're in for a treat. My mother makes the best Norwegian meatballs you've ever tasted. She adds just a pinch of nutmeg and allspice to bring out the full flavor. You'll love it."

The bright lights of the house beckoned. Laughter and music drifted from the open windows, and stepping across the threshold, they were swept up into the party. Jordan immediately caught sight of Thor. He stood in the middle of a crowd, reminding her of all she preferred to forget. Vaguely threatened, Jordan looked away.

Where's your fighting spirit now? she asked herself sardonically. *One look at Andrea's thunder god and you're cowering in Rainer's arms.* Her lips curved upward. But what a pair of arms in which to cower!

Brita's voice hailed her. "Jordan, I hoped I'd see you tonight." She came rushing up to them. "Have you met Father yet?"

"We just arrived," Rainer said.

"Mom's in the kitchen. Come say hello." Brita wrinkled her nose at her brother. "You don't mind if I steal your date for a few minutes?"

Not waiting for an answer, she whisked Jordan off. "You look great," she chattered. "It's fun to have an opportunity to dress up, isn't it? I get tired of jeans and T-shirts after a while." She pointed to the strand of pearls encircling Jordan's neck. "I like those."

"They were my mother's. So were the earrings." She tossed her hair back over her shoulder and touched the matching pearl studs.

"Nice." Brita pushed open the door to the huge crowded kitchen. Food covered practically every available surface. In the middle of the bustle stood Sonja, her height and pale blond hair unmistakable.

The older woman greeted Jordan with a warm smile. "Welcome. Have you had *middag*—dinner? It's buffet style tonight, so help yourself. Brita, get her a plate and cup. Knowing Rainer, she's probably starved."

Jordan stood off to one side, quite happy to listen to the teasing happy group, Norwegian phrases and words mingled readily with English.

"So what have you decided about Cornucopia?" Brita asked. "Are we at war yet?"

"Not yet," Jordan said noncommittally.

Sonja interrupted sternly. "No shoptalk. Here." She shoved a platter into her daughter's hands. "Take this out to the living room. And make sure Leo gets some of that *Rommegrøt*. He especially asked for it."

"Put my foot in my mouth again, did I?" Brita flashed Jordan a teasing grin. "Then, I'm off. My mother's a firm believer in idle hands and Satan's mischief and all that. I'll be back as soon as I take this dessert porridge out to Mr. Goldbrick." She disappeared through the door, tray in hand.

The name Brita mentioned flagged a memory. "Leo Goldbrick?" Jordan said aloud.

Sonja glanced over and nodded. "Do you know him?"

"He owned a market in White Center, didn't he?" she temporized.

"That's right. We bought him out a few years back."

Jordan couldn't hide her surprise. "But I heard..."

"That we put him out of business?"

Reluctantly she nodded. "I understood you opened a competing market across the street from him."

"We did," the older woman replied easily. "Rumor must not have told you we bought Leo out first. We opted for a new location, instead of taking over his existing store."

Jordan looked at her in confusion. "Then how did the rumors start?"

"Because poor Leo was reluctant to abandon his market, even though he'd been eager to sell. And Rainer being Rainer—" his mother shrugged "—he let Leo take his time closing down."

Which meant he wasn't the villain she'd originally thought, Jordan realized with relief. Andrea had the story wrong. What else might her friend have gotten wrong? It certainly put a whole new complexion on things. "He's not so ruthless after all," she murmured.

Sonja laughed, not unkindly. "Don't kid yourself. The Thorsens are a ruthless lot, all right. You live with it, or stay clear. I live with it."

"Why are they like that?" Jordan had to ask.

Sonja shrugged. "Thor has his own reasons for being, well, Thor. With Rainer it's because he takes his responsibilities so seriously. If it's in the best interest of the family, he can be merciless."

Jordan looked down at the crumbs on her empty plate, struggling to conceal her alarm. Sonja only confirmed what Rainer had told her earlier. It shouldn't come as any surprise. If only he'd understand. By putting Cornucopia out of business, he would destroy the very thing the Thorsens held so dear—family and tradition.

She looked up and saw Rainer making his way through the crowd. His eyes met hers, their gazes locking. In that moment she knew she loved him. The knowledge hurt like hell, but she wouldn't change it for all the apples in Yakima. The ferocity of her need burned within her, the futility of her desire turning it to ashes.

For despite her love, Cornucopia still stood between them.

"SO WHAT'S WRONG?" Rainer asked her on the way home.

Jordan stared out the window. "What could be wrong?"

"Make a list. Do we head it with the Thorsens or Cornucopia?"

We head it with the fact that I love you, she almost said. "I'm sorry. I didn't mean to put a damper on things." She forced enthusiasm into her voice. "Everyone was very nice. I like your father. I didn't realize he used a wheelchair."

"He broke his back fifteen years ago." Rainer frowned. "You're avoiding my question. What's wrong?"

Jordan bowed her head, her tone reserved. "I've been thinking about this whole situation." She sighed. "And I don't see any way out."

The warning lights on the Ballard Bridge began to blink and a gate lowered, blocking the road. Rainer pulled to a stop and cut the car engine. Jordan spotted the mast of a sailboat, waiting for the center spans of the bridge to lift and allow it passage. Without a word, she opened the door and jumped out, crossing to the pedestrian walkway. Peering over the edge, she watched the sailboat angle into the middle of the canal.

Rainer joined her. He put an arm around her waist, pulling her close. "It'll all work out. Give it time."

"How?" Jordan set her jaw. "By our bowing down to the mighty Thorsens? By Cornucopia acquiring another name—Thorsen's North, perhaps?"

"Possibly. Or possibly not. What does Cletus think?"

She wanted to laugh. "He thinks you'll pay to work for us forever. Or that he'll wake up one day and you'll have gone, and his problems will be solved."

"Incredible." The two sides of the bridge stretched high into the night sky and the sailboat began to drift through the open spans. "I'm sorry you're the one left with all the worries, Jordan. I wish—" He broke off without completing his sentence.

"Me, too," she whispered.

The bridge began to close, and they turned and walked back to the car. Rainer drove the rest of the way without speaking. In too short a time, he pulled into her driveway.

"The back?" he suggested. At her nod, he drove around to the rear of the house. He parked and got out, circling the car to open her door. "Thanks for coming tonight." He put his arm around her shoulders and walked with her across the neglected lawn of knee-high grass.

"I really should cut this," she murmured, embarrassed.

"Right. Sometime after work ends at midnight and before it begins at five in the morning, you should be out here with your mower."

"Okay, so I'll hire someone." She laughed, leaning against him. "Like to earn five bucks?"

He looked down at her and chuckled. Then the humor died from his face, his expression turning serious. "Jordan, I—"

Whatever he'd been about to say was interrupted by a loud infuriated caterwauling. Scratch, clearly objecting to Rainer's foot taking up residence on his tail, decided to live up to his name. Ten razor-sharp claws sank into Rainer's ankle.

With a muffled oath, Rainer hopped up and down in the deep dew-laden grass, trying to shake the cat off. The cat proved his tenacity by hanging on—and digging in.

"Rainer, no! Don't grab me or we'll—" her feet slid out from under her and she fell, bringing Rainer and the cat down with her "—slip," she finished, shoving at his shoulders. "Did anyone ever tell you you're heavy?"

"It's not me, it's the cat. He's on my back— Ouch!"

With a final indignant meow, Scratch parted company with them. He stalked toward Rainer's car, only the tip of his tail visible above the tall grass. With a single perfect leap he landed on the bright red hood and sat, calmly cleaning his paws.

"I'd get up and kill that cat if I wasn't so comfortable," Rainer said. He braced himself on his elbows.

Jordan took a deep breath, instantly recognizing her mistake. Every inch of her pushed against every inch of him. Her body fit his in perfect alignment, an alignment that felt perfectly marvelous. She stared up at him, her eyes wide with wonder.

Rainer smiled. "Feels good doesn't it?" He brushed her hair back from her face. His lean fingers and her thick dark curls and the long sweet grass became deliciously entangled. Taking his time, he sketched a path from her cheek, along the pearls encircling her neck, to the strap of her dress. He hesitated briefly, then eased it slowly to one side, baring her shoulder. His hand spread across the exposed skin, his fingers stroking her with a light delicate touch.

"Rainer," she moaned. "Someone will see."

His lips replaced his hands. "No one will see us. The grass is too long."

"Uncle Cletus—"

He nipped the curve of her shoulder, his tongue caressing the slight indentations. "—is probably asleep. Like the rest of the world. They're all asleep, except us."

Jordan trembled, desire slipping beneath her defenses, invading and conquering. Her heart pounded against her ribs and she strained to draw breath. A burning heat gathered in the pit of her stomach and she wished with an intensity born of desperation that they were someplace else, someplace where they could assuage this urgent need building within them.

Rainer pushed himself up, the muscles of his forearms bulging with the effort. For several long compelling seconds, he studied her flushed face, then slowly, so slowly she thought she'd die before he reached her, he lowered himself back down. Finally his lips found hers.

Her mouth parted beneath his, welcoming him. She put her hands on his waist, thrusting them beneath the cotton polo shirt he wore. The heat of his skin practically blistered her palms. She ran her hands along his rib cage, lingering over the hard sculpted muscles of his chest and shoulders.

She squirmed down into the grass, the uneven ground hard against her back. A low rumbling noise sounded near her ear. Startled, she dragged her mouth from Rainer's.

"What's that?" she whispered. She turned her head and looked directly into the unblinking stare of Scratch. His rumbling grew louder, and she realized in astonishment that he was purring.

Rainer muttered a curse and swatted at the cat. It was a major mistake.

An earsplitting howl erupted from the indignant animal. An instant later the back-porch light flickered on.

"What's all that noise? What's going on there?" Uncle Cletus called out.

"Don't make a sound. Maybe he'll go away," Rainer whispered in her ear. Obediently Jordan kept quiet.

"Jordan? Is that you? What are you doing on the lawn there? Have you hurt yourself, girl?"

Rainer rolled off her and she sat up, brushing bits of grass and twigs from her hair. "Uh...no. Not exactly."

Walker poked his head out from behind Cletus, observing them with an unblinking stare identical to the cat's. He held a papaya in one hand and a passion fruit in the other. "Huh," he said.

Uncle Cletus glared at him. "You don't have to overstate the matter." He cleared his throat. "Being a traditional sort of man," he announced, "I'll assume the best and close the door."

"What's the best?" Rainer muttered from beside her.

"You don't want to know," she assured him.

"I'm closing the door now. Walker and I will just go on with our checker game, and you can go on with..." He appeared slightly nonplussed. "I'm closing the door." And finally did so.

"Dare I ask what we do now?" Rainer asked.

"You daren't. I have maybe ten seconds to get in there if our reputations are to avoid—"

"Being sullied?"

"More like being further sullied." She started to reach for him, but stopped herself in time. "And as much as I like the idea of your sullying me, this is neither the time nor the place."

Rainer stood up and offered her his hand, pulling her to her feet. "Come with me tomorrow, then." He began brushing the bits of grass and dirt from her dress. Diligently. By the time he'd finished, she was trembling so much she could hardly stand. "The store's closed Sunday. We could have all day. Alone. Together."

She didn't give herself time to think. "Yes," she said quickly, before she could dream up a thousand reasons to say no. She glanced at the back door and then stood on tiptoe, planting a swift kiss on his lips. He didn't let her get away with it. He swept her into a tight embrace and gave her a kiss she could dream about for a long time to come.

Jordan practically floated into the house, her uncle's expression bringing her down to earth with a thump.

"You two are getting awful cozy," he said in disapproving tones. "Just where is all *that*—" he gestured toward the back lawn "—leading?"

"Where?" Walker echoed.

Guilt swamped her. What had she been thinking of? How could she have forgotten Cornucopia and Uncle Cletus and Walker? "Don't you worry," she assured her uncle stoutly. "My loyalties are with you through thick and thin."

"Hmph," he snorted. "More like thin and thin."

"Hmph," Walker added.

Slowly Jordan climbed the steps to her bedroom. One week remained of Rainer's time at Cornucopia, she realized dismally. One week to reach an agreement—something they weren't even close to accomplishing, despite their growing relationship. The problem was, she couldn't sell out, and the only way for Rainer to win was to drive them out. Either way, their relationship would be ruined.

She slumped down on her bed. She still had tomorrow's date with him. If she was smart, she'd enjoy their few remaining hours, because they'd soon be over. For come week's end, he'd be out of her life permanently. To her utter astonishment, a solitary tear crept down her cheek.

JORDAN SLIPPED OUT of the house at the crack of dawn. She intended to make the most of her day with Rainer. By unspoken agreement, Uncle Cletus and Cornucopia weren't mentioned.

"Where to first?" Rainer asked.

"Let's go into Seattle and walk down by the piers," she suggested. "We can have breakfast and then stroll through Pike's Place Market. I'd like to look at the produce stands there and compare prices and quality."

"Can't resist, can you?"

She gave him an impish grin. "No."

"And the fish markets? Shall we pick up some crab or gooey duck?"

She considered it, then shook her head. "Not today. Because after Pike's, I thought we'd wander around Myrtle Edwards Park and then ride the ferry to Bainbridge Island."

"Full day you have planned there."

Their gazes met and locked. "I want a full day with you," she said. *It might be our last,* she added to herself.

He nodded. "Then let's get at it."

Walking along the nearly empty piers fronting Puget Sound worked up their appetites. By mutual consent, they stuffed themselves on hot buttery cinnamon rolls while they wandered through Pike's Place Market.

The vendors there were fiercely competitive, and Jordan studied their stalls with equal parts envy and scorn. They displayed their produce beautifully, she'd give them that, and the quality was top-notch. But none of these stalls came close to comparing with the beauty and distinctiveness of Cornucopia.

Several of the vendors called out greetings, and more than a few seemed astonished to see Jordan and Rainer together. One of the hawkers tossed them each an apple. With smiles of thanks, they moved on to examine the crafts booths.

At a jeweler's stall Jordan's eye was caught by a dainty solid-gold tomato charm. The stem and leaf curled down onto the vegetable, forming a loop for the chain.

It reminded her of the day Rainer first visited Cornucopia—and the double-edged conversation they'd conducted with Mrs. Swenson. She remembered his hands, moving with exquisite delicacy over the plump red tomato. She shivered, staring at the trinket for a long time.

They lunched at an open-air restaurant down by the piers, dining on crab salads and sharing a bottle of locally made wine. Jordan couldn't take her eyes off Rainer. She loved him. That hopeless knowledge haunted her, filling her with sorrow. But she found she didn't regret her feelings.

It was a moment out of time and she knew he savored it every bit as much as she. The afternoon flew by. They rode the trolley cars, strolled through Myrtle Edwards Park and sat in the grass, watching the ferries make their leisurely way back and forth across Puget Sound.

After a spaghetti dinner they headed for Pier 52 and boarded the ferry for Bainbridge Island. The moon, still full and benevolent, glowed down on them as they stood in the bow. Jordan huddled in the protective warmth of Rainer's arms, knowing there was no place on earth she'd rather be.

He reached into his pocket and to her astonishment pulled out the gold tomato charm. Without a word, he fastened it around her neck. Then he kissed her, with only the moon and the stars looking on. Jordan knew she'd remember that moment for the rest of her life.

The ferry returned them to Seattle just after midnight, and they decided to call it a day. Walking arm in arm, Jordan snuggled against Rainer, touching her charm with gentle fingers.

"I'll meet you at Constantine's," Rainer confirmed on the drive home. "You're going to be beat. I almost regret keeping you out so late." He pulled in front of her house and switched off the engine.

"I don't." She slid closer to him, wrapping her arms about his neck. "I can sleep any time."

THE DAYS FLEW BY. All Jordan could think about was Rainer, and the swift passage of time, and the threat that stood between them. She worried constantly and slept little. She knew it showed in both the darkening circles beneath her eyes and in her forced cheerfulness.

She had to find a way out of this mess. She clutched her tomato charm as though for inspiration. *If only I had an angle. Just one.* But nothing came to her.

Releasing the charm, she pushed her hair back from her face, looking around. At least setup continued to go well. That should count for something. The employees rarely fought, Uncle Cletus hadn't mentioned politics in days, and Walker actually smiled. So why couldn't she be happy with that?

Rainer's voice interrupted her musing. "Jordan, did you hear what I said?"

She looked at him blankly. "What?"

"I said, there's a huge crowd starting to gather outside. What gives?"

It took her several moments to understand what he meant. Finally, clasping her by the shoulders, he steered her to the front of the store. There she found an ever-growing line of customers waiting impatiently for Cornucopia to open.

"Oh. It must be Wednesday. Our ad broke today."

"What ad?"

"We decided to run some ads to see if we couldn't..."

"Circumvent the Thorsen threat?" he suggested.

She smiled weakly. "Something like that." She glanced at the crowd, a small frown wrinkling her brow. "I know we have some good prices, but this is better than I ever dreamed. Okay, everybody," she called out. "Let's get ready. We're going to be very busy this morning."

She opened the door to a veritable tidal wave of people. Knowing Michelle and Uncle Cletus couldn't handle the registers on their own, she manned a third one. Within minutes a woman she'd never served before approached her counter, two baskets in hand, one overflowing with grapes, the other with nectarines.

"I couldn't believe my eyes when I saw your ad this morning," she gasped, setting down her burden. "I decided to give your store a try and rushed right over before you ran out."

Jordan smiled. "Not much chance of that."

She glanced at the woman's basket, a little disappointed that it contained only sale items. She wished she could have tempted her new customer with a few things not on special. Jordan brightened. Maybe the woman would come again. Maybe she'd start coming on a regular basis.

"I'm glad you're pleased with us," Jordan said with a friendly smile. She pulled out the plastic bags filled with grapes. "I thought fifty-nine cents a pound on these would be an excellent buy."

The woman laughed. "Sure it would. But offering them at nineteen cents a pound is an unbeatable one."

Jordan stared at her. "What?"

"Nineteen cents a pound," the woman repeated, her voice rising a notch. "That's what your ad says." She reached into her purse and whipped out a newspaper, spreading it open to the appropriate page. She thumped a stubby finger against the bold print.

"It's right here in black and white. Grapes. Nineteen cents a pound. Nectarines. Twenty-nine cents a pound. Tomatoes. Ten cents a pound." The woman directed a stony look at Jordan. "If I didn't grow my own tomatoes, I'd have a basketful of those, as well."

The newspaper blurred before Jordan's eyes and a dawning sense of disbelief and dread crept over her. The ad. The ad Uncle Cletus took care of for her so she could go out with Rainer. The ad she was supposed to check—and hadn't. *Because she'd been so distracted by Rainer.*

"Th-there must be some mistake," Jordan stuttered.

"There sure is if you don't plan on honoring your ad prices," the woman agreed, her voice rising another notch. Several of the customers stopped what they were doing and turned to stare at the commotion. "You *are* going to honor your own ad, aren't you? I don't think you'll be in business much longer if you don't."

The store grew rapidly quieter. Jordan slipped her hands under the counter and balled them into tight fists to control their shaking.

"Of course we honor our ads. I—I was just surprised there'd be such interest," she lied valiantly.

Rainer came to stand beside her. "What's up?" he murmured.

"Everything's fine," she replied in an undertone, reaching for her charm. "There's been a small mix-up with the ad."

He gave her a long hard look. "What can I do?"

"Keep us stocked." A tiny break in her voice betrayed her anxiety. She knew Rainer noticed, but he didn't say anything. With a quick nod, he headed for the cooler, calling to Andy and Leroy.

Jordan struggled to keep her panic at bay. What was she going to do? Thinking about the amount of money they stood to lose horrified her. She quickly added up the woman's purchases, and the next woman's—again ad items only—and slipped the piddling amount of money she received into the cash drawer. Within an hour, she realized demand would far outstrip their inventory.

"Andy," she called out, "take over the register." She hurried to the back of the store where Rainer and Leroy and Walker worked as hard and fast as they could to keep everything stocked. "I've got to make a run down to Constantine's," she announced, avoiding Rainer's gaze.

"No," he insisted. "What you have to do is stop this nonsense, now, before it's too late. We can put up signs, explaining the newspaper made an error. People will understand."

She lifted her head and looked him straight in the eye. "The newspaper didn't make a mistake," she said. "I did." And it was the truth. Not checking that ad had been *her* error. "I have a reputation to maintain. Which means I honor our ad and keep us fully stocked—no matter what the cost."

Without another word, she left the store and climbed into her truck. For a brief minute she rested her head against the steering wheel, the enormity of her situation threatening to overwhelm her. How would she get out of this mess? Fumbling for her charm again, she stiffened her spine. Somehow she would work her way out, just as she always did.

Yanking out the choke, she fired up the truck. She had a job to do.

CHAPTER NINE

AT THE CLOSE of business Wednesday evening, Jordan looked around at the shambles once known as Cornucopia. Never, in all the fifty years of its existence, had it been in such a state. Bitter awareness filled her, and the muscles in her jaw tightened. By putting her own concerns first, she'd let the family down. It was her responsibility to protect the store, and she'd failed.

She'd always thought of Cornucopia as her past and her future. She smiled without humor. It didn't look like much of a future now.

Her gaze moved over the room. She took in the ripped table skirts, the mangled grapes and stems scattered on the floor, the pile of bruised nectarines and the sagging tomato table. She groaned. The tomato table—built with her father's own two hands—had actually broken beneath the press of customers and the weight of the vegetables. Fortunately Rainer managed to shore it up. Temporarily. She shut her eyes, unable to look further.

This...this *ruin* represented the Roberts name. And she'd disgraced it. If she'd given more thought—even a single thought—to Cornucopia's needs instead of her own, this wouldn't have happened. But instead, she'd been caught up in her passion and desire for Rainer. Thoughts of him dominated every waking and sleeping moment. She'd gotten her priorities mixed, and this was the result.

She glanced over at Leroy and Andy and Michelle. They were so exhausted they could barely stand. It only added to her guilt. "Come on back to the lunchroom," she told them. "I have sodas in the fridge. Help yourselves."

They exchanged disheartened looks, then nodded reluctantly, trooping in unison to the back of the store. She'd better come up with something fast, or there'd be three less employees tomorrow, Jordan realized. These kids didn't look like they could handle one more day like today, let alone three. Her head dropped forward. If only she weren't so bone weary. If only she could think straight.

Coward! she taunted. *Spineless wonder! If you can't face life's occasional adversities, then you don't deserve Cornucopia. Now get up and fight, or give it up and go slither under some rock.*

It took a full thirty seconds of concentrated effort to force her muscles to obey her silent commands. Gritting her teeth, she threw back her shoulders and stood up straight. It took an additional thirty seconds to smooth down her hair, adjust her wrinkled clothing and affix a decisive I'm-in-charge-and-can-handle-this expression on her face.

She managed—barely.

Jordan walked into the lunchroom and gazed at her war-weary troops. The three younger employees sat slumped over the table, nursing sodas. Walker, his mouth sagging open, snoozed in a corner. Uncle Cletus leaned against the wall, his face a sickly shade of gray. She took a deep breath, forcing a cheerful note into her voice.

"Well, I've got some good news and some bad news." Moans met her statement.

She crossed the room to the refrigerator, helping herself to a cola. Thank goodness for caffeine! She popped open the lid and took a deep swallow. "Why don't we get the bad news over with first," she said with a bright smile.

"We're all fired and you're giving us two weeks' severance pay?" Andy suggested hopefully.

" 'Fraid not." She saw Rainer walk in and stand by the door. It took all her concentration to ignore him and continue speaking. "The bad news is the ad prices in today's paper don't expire until Saturday. We can expect three more days like today."

"Three?" Michelle repeated in alarm. She swallowed, rallying with an effort. "We can survive that, can't we?"

"Yeah," muttered Andy and Leroy in unison, though they sounded far from positive.

Jordan winced. If only they didn't look so crushed. She didn't think she'd lose her employees, but they deserved better than this. Desperate times called for desperate measures. "The good news is you'll all get a bonus for those three days."

That seemed to cheer them. Then Michelle glanced at the other two and whispered something beneath her breath. Andy and Leroy nodded. "Forget it," she said. "It's nice of you to offer, but you don't have to pay us extra. We've decided and we're with you on this. You know—ups and downs, good and bad, awful and worse."

Tears pricked Jordan's eyes. "Thanks," she murmured. "You guys are the best."

Rainer shifted and she peeked at him through lowered lashes. He stood, expressionless, a shoulder propped against the doorjamb, his arms folded across his chest: the Viking at his Viking-est. Disapproval, clear and powerful, radiated from him. But surprisingly he remained silent.

Jordan turned her attention to her employees. "Thanks for understanding. We'll discuss this further another time." She touched Michelle's shoulder. "Why don't you three take off. Be back bright and early tomorrow. It's going to be a rough few days."

Apparently they agreed. As one, they rose and headed out the door, murmuring among themselves.

Uncle Cletus shifted in his chair. She'd never seen him look so uncomfortable. "Looks like we've gotten ourselves in a bit of a pickle. Can we handle it?"

"Of course we can handle it." She tried for an encouraging smile. "We'll manage just fine."

"This is all my fault," he fussed. "I don't understand what went wrong."

Jordan tried to reassure him. "It's all right, Uncle Cletus. I guess I didn't make the numbers clear enough."

"Clear," Walker said, now wide awake. "Very clear."

Uncle Cletus fidgeted nervously, rubbing a hand across his bald spot. "Walker's right," he admitted. "Your numbers were clear enough. It was just...just..." His face puckered into a frown. "You said we should run loser ads. Fifty-nine cents a pound for grapes wasn't much of a loser. So I thought...if we could get more customers by cropping our prices a *little*..." His voice trailed off miserably.

Jordan shut her eyes. *Oh, Uncle Cletus, what have you done?* He wanted to help, that's all, she tried to convince herself. Unfortunately his business acumen had gone downhill since his stroke. She knew that. She should have protected him.

"Forget it," she said. "Things aren't too bad. Andrea promised to sell us the ad items at cost. That should help. And we don't know yet how many new customers we've gained."

Cletus looked up, renewed hope in his eyes. "It'll all work out, won't it?"

"Of course it will." She smiled encouragingly. "We may have to tighten our belts a little, but it isn't anything we can't handle—given time."

"Tighten our belts?" Cletus repeated in dismay. He rose to his feet, his expression one of bewilderment. "But I wear suspenders."

Jordan bit her tongue. "Why don't you and Walker go over to the house and have a game of checkers," she suggested. "I've got a few things to do around here, and then I'll be over. Okay?"

"I'll do that," he said. Walker stood up and together the two men left, Uncle Cletus muttering to himself about loosening belts and tightening suspenders.

Rainer pushed away from the doorjamb before she could make good her escape, blocking the exit. "We've got a few things to discuss," he said.

She had a good idea what those few things might be, and no way on this planet did she intend to discuss them. "I have work to do. It'll have to wait." She attempted to brush by him and he caught her arm.

"We'll discuss them now."

She considered arguing, but flat out didn't have the strength. Defeated, she nodded. "Fine. Start discussing."

He released her arm and drew a deep breath. "You have some loyal employees who are willing to stick by you. I'm impressed. But why whitewash things for your uncle? He's the one who caused this mess. It's his store. Why isn't he the one taking responsibility?"

"I take on the responsibility because it's my job," she insisted. "Uncle Cletus made an error in judgment. That's all. Besides, what good would harping at him do? Would it change the facts? No. Would it make me feel better to beat him into the ground? No. I look at the bottom line and go from there. I figure out how to keep our employees, how to mitigate damages, and how to turn this whole ugly mess to our advantage."

A humorless smile lit his face. "If you come up with a way to turn *this* to your advantage, let me know."

"I will. In the meantime, I have work to do. Either get out of my way, or get run over. It's your choice."

She'd never seen his eyes so dark and threatening. "You have a funny way of asking for help, love."

Damn her pride! And damn the family loyalty that forced her to say, "There's nothing to keep you here. This isn't your business, Rainer. I appreciate all you did today, but you don't have to stay."

With all her heart, she hoped he would. But she'd learned the hard way that what she hoped and what she wanted didn't matter in the least.

"Now there you're wrong, sweetheart. I do have to stay," he said through gritted teeth. "I paid five hundred dollars for the privilege, remember?" His voice lowered ominously. "And don't you dare offer to refund the money."

"Don't worry. I can't," she said, her tone dry as dust. "Unless you want it in tomatoes."

For a brief instant, amusement flickered in his deep green eyes. Then it was gone. "Let's get busy. We've got a long night ahead of us."

She hesitated. "Rainer, I . . ." The words wouldn't come. "Thanks," she said in a thick voice. "I owe you."

Not only did it turn out to be a long night setting the store to rights, it turned out be a *very* long night. Jordan finally crawled into bed at two in the morning, feeling like one massive raw nerve. She didn't know how she'd survive the rest of the week. It would take every bit of grit and determination she possessed and then some. But she'd manage. Somehow. Cornucopia would survive, even if it killed her. She rolled over, her muscles protesting the movement. And kill her it probably would.

OVER THE NEXT TWO DAYS, Jordan discovered the meaning of the word *hell*. The seemingly endless hours passed in a blur of work and exhaustion—but never tears. She refused to give in to the luxury. She barely exchanged half a dozen words with Rainer. She knew he was worried. But she had the family honor to uphold. What else did he expect her to do?

Jordan sighed. She knew what he expected. He expected her to give in. He expected her to sell out. But she wouldn't. Locking the doors Friday night, she could hardly contain her relief. One more day. She could survive another twenty-four hours—she hoped.

Grabbing a wooden box of radishes, she headed for the cooler. Two steps later the box slipped from her grasp and crashed to the floor. She stood and stared at it, too tired to bend over and pick it up. Too tired to care.

Rainer appeared behind her and lifted her bodily out of the way. "Odin's blood! There's nothing left to grab. I could knock you over with a kiss."

Jordan closed her eyes, shivering at the thought. She'd love to be knocked over by his kiss. She'd missed being held by him and kissed by him... Deliberately she pushed the thought away. She couldn't give into *that* luxury any more than she could tears.

"I'll survive," she muttered.

"I'm not so sure." He bent down and tossed the radishes into the box.

Her mouth tightened. "I can handle it."

"Maybe. But why should you?" He stood and glared at her. "Cletus owns the store. It was his mistake. When does he take responsibility for his own actions? And when are you going to stop covering for him? He should know what he's doing to you."

"He's not doing anything to me," she snapped back. "It's my choice. If I'd checked the ad in the first place, none of this would have happened."

"That's almost too ludicrous to comment on—" He slammed the radishes onto the counter. "No! I will comment, if only because it should be said aloud. He's a grown man, Jordan. If he can't handle the business or if his health interferes, then he should get out. What happens when he retires? You'll have to take on his work, as well. You'll never have a life to call your own. You don't now!"

"Just because I haven't time for a roll in the...in the grass with you, doesn't mean I don't have a life. I have a life right here. It's a very satisfying one."

He stepped closer. "So I see. So satisfying that you've dropped five pounds." His hand closed over her wrist and he groaned. "What's happened to my Valkyrie? She's fading away right in front of me."

She made a small murmur of denial and attempted to pull free.

He cupped her face, holding her, his thumbs brushing across her cheekbones. "Your eyes—so shadowed and empty. They aren't blue anymore, or gray. There aren't any typhoons left, no more volcanoes, no fire and brimstone—just sheer exhaustion. Jordan, look at what you're doing. Look beyond Cornucopia. Look at what else could be part of your life."

"You mean you," she said. "Forget it! You're what got me into this mess in the first place."

He stilled, his expression alert and wary. "What are you talking about?"

She trembled within his grasp, too angry and exhausted to choose her words. "I was so distracted by you I neglected my job and my family—worse, I neglected Cornucopia. I'd have remembered to check that ad if I hadn't been so busy playing Viking love games.''

"You don't really believe that, do you?''

"Yes, I do! You're right. I can't have both Cornucopia and a relationship in my life. At least, not right now.''

"Meaning?''

"Meaning one or the other goes.''

"So now you choose.'' He said it without inflection, which made it all the more final.

Her chin lifted defiantly. "All right, I choose. And I choose Cornucopia.'' She thought her heart would break as she said the words. But family had to come first. Cornucopia had to come first. "Stay away tomorrow,'' she told him, though it sounded more like a plea. "Give us some time to weigh our options. Give *me* some time.''

He thought about it and nodded with reluctance. "Very well, I'll stay away.'' He gave her a direct look. "But only until Monday. By Monday, this whole business will be resolved.''

JORDAN MADE IT through Saturday, though just. Without Rainer's physical and emotional support, she quickly found herself in over her head. Sheer perversity kept her from folding until the last customer had left. Then she took the sorry amount of money in the cash register, locked Cornucopia and trudged home.

She should deposit the money at the bank, she argued with herself. It wasn't safe keeping it around the house. With a yawn that practically knocked her over, she shoved the sack of change, bills and checks under her pillow, fell on top of it, and was asleep before her feet left the floor.

Sunday afternoon at one, Jordan finally awoke. With Uncle Cletus nowhere to be found, she made a fast run to the bank before going over to the store. Not giving herself time to think about the disaster that awaited, she started at one end and worked steadily to the other, cleaning everything in sight.

That done, she wandered restlessly through the market, feeling at loose ends. If only she could release some of her excess tension. She brightened. Maybe she'd give herself a treat and check out the other groceries in the area—compare prices and quality. It was another facet of her job, and one she particularly enjoyed. She locked up quickly and headed for the national chain store down the street.

Within minutes, the feeling of stress drained away. Taking her time, she examined everything, and by the end of her walk-through, she'd satisfied herself that Cornucopia was the better store. Naturally. Just as she turned to leave, she glimpsed Seth, the student who always shopped at Cornucopia—her "personal project," as she liked to think of him.

Jordan smiled, about to approach, when she spotted the fruits and vegetables loaded in his cart. Her smile faded. Wait a minute. What was he doing? He couldn't afford that. He was a penniless student forced to shop at Cornucopia on credit. He'd always needed a helping hand—*her* helping hand. How could he pay for all that food? She frowned in confusion.

Just then a produce worker came out of the storage area behind her, pushing a trolley loaded with cabbage. Jordan lowered her head, pretending an intense interest in the alfalfa sprouts.

"Hiya, Seth," the store employee said in a friendly voice. "Not shopping at Cornucopia today?"

Seth shook his head. "They're closed. Besides, I have to be careful. If my tab gets too high there, I might actually have to pay it!"

The produce man laughed. "Which is why we don't offer credit. After all, business is business."

Jordan stood there stunned, unable to believe what she'd just heard. Her most loyal customer wasn't loyal at all! Not in the least. He'd been using her, taking advantage of her generosity, just as Michelle and Rainer had suggested. He didn't shop at Cornucopia because the market was special. He did it because she never forced him to pay! How blind she'd been.

"Business is business," the produce man had said. And he was right. Cornucopia—something she'd considered in the same light as a family member—was a *business*. Her parents and grandparents wouldn't want her to sacrifice everything for Cornucopia. Nor did they live on through the store, as she'd always thought. Their accomplishments and their memory lived on through her. For the past ten years, she'd put business before everything else in her life—even before her own happiness.

Even before Rainer.

No longer, she decided then and there. She refused to be blinded to the truth for another minute. She wanted more from life than a store. She wanted love and a family. Mostly she wanted Rainer. And she didn't intend losing him. Though she'd fight to keep the market, if it came to a choice, Cornucopia would lose. Hands down.

Which left her to make some decisions about the future. She thought about Rainer's suggestion—to look beyond Cornucopia at what else could be part of her life. He'd made a valid point.

She felt a huge weight lift from her shoulders. Rainer had known all along that Cornucopia hung like an albatross around her neck. But she'd carried the responsibility for so long she didn't know how freedom felt. Until now. If she lost the market, her life wouldn't end. She'd find something else to do. She grinned. Of course she would.

She left the chain store and returned home. The house stood dark and empty. Where was Uncle Cletus? she wondered. Her stomach growled in hunger and she headed for the kitchen to fix a quick omelet. There, she found his note:

Have errands to run. Don't worry about the store, I'll take care of everything. Wake me before you leave tomorrow. Love you, girl.

U.C.

"I love you, too," she murmured. "And you don't have to worry about a thing. I've taken care of it for you. And I always will."

The next morning, Jordan peeked into her uncle's bedroom—he looked exhausted. Deciding not to disturb him, she quietly closed the door. She'd talk to him after buying. Things should be a lot quieter at Cornucopia this morning.

She left the house in renewed spirits, feeling good about yesterday's decisions. The August morning had dawned bright and fresh, the sea gulls and crows as raucous as ever. She hopped in the truck and drove south toward the city. Rainer had mentioned Monday as his personal deadline. Did he plan to meet her at the wholesale market? The thought gave her a warm happy glow. She urged a little more speed out of the truck.

The docks bustled with normal Monday morning traffic. She climbed the steps to the loading area, and the noise and confusion abated. She looked around, surprised by the sudden silence. Was she being paranoid, or did it have something to do with her?

After a momentary uneasiness, she waved to Marco and another salesman, Mel, who were busy writing up an order for a small stand in Lake City. They stared at her. Hesitantly Marco raised his hand. Then he spoke sharply to Mel, snapped closed his order book and hurried off the docks into Constantine's warehouse. Mel gave her one final curious glance and went back to work.

Okay, so she'd been a little out of sorts last week, Jordan admitted grudgingly. She frowned. Maybe more than a little. But had she been such a terror that they couldn't stand being on the same dock with her?

She stepped into the warehouse, looking for Terry, and discovered him off to one side talking to Marco. The two argued, gestures flying in every direction. The discussion ended abruptly, with Marco barking out a final heated comment and scuttling toward the steps that led to the offices. Terry turned and approached.

"What? Do I have leprosy or something?" she groused good-naturedly. "I know I was a little bit temperamental last week, but—"

"What are you doing here, Jordan? I thought you'd be home."

She stared at him in bewilderment. "Why would I be home? I have buying to do. Have you ever known me to miss a day?"

He yanked his cap low over his brow, refusing to meet her eyes. "No," he muttered. "But that was before—" he shrugged "—you know."

"No, I don't know. Why don't you fill me in?" He looked everywhere but at her, humming and hawing. She tapped her foot impatiently. Enough was enough. "Now, come on," she began in a no-nonsense voice.

Before Jordan could get another word out, she heard someone hailing her from a second-floor office window. Andrea's timing was, as usual, uncanny. "Come up and see me. I need to talk to you."

Jordan glanced at Terry, noting his relief—and wondering. "I gather the boss lady will explain?"

He couldn't have looked more miserable. Pulling out a checkered handkerchief, he mopped the back of his neck. "I'm sorry," he mumbled. "Real sorry. I wish there was something...ah, shoot." He shoved the hanky into his back pocket. "See ya 'round," he said, and took off.

Real alarm raced through her. What the heck was going on? Had Nick blown his cork because Andrea had sold them their ad items at cost? Maybe her family was no longer welcome at Constantine's. She stared up at Andrea's office, seeing the tall blonde standing at the window, an unusually grim expression on her face.

Taking a deep breath, Jordan headed for the steps. She climbed them two at a time, striding down the hallway to her friend's office. She opened the door without knocking and stepped inside.

"Okay, what gives?" she demanded without preliminary.

Andrea crossed the room and shut the door. "Sit down, Jordan."

"I don't want to sit down. I want to know—"

"Sit down!" Andrea closed her eyes. "Please."

Jordan shoved a stack of papers off the chair and, without another word, obeyed. "Okay. I'm sitting. Now will you tell me what's wrong?"

"When's the last time you saw your uncle?" Andrea asked unexpectedly.

Jordan leapt to her feet. "Uncle Cletus? What's happened to him? Is he all right?"

Andrea put her hands on Jordan's shoulders and pressed her back into the chair. "Take it easy. As far as I'm aware your uncle's *physical* health is just fine. I've never been able to swear to his mental well-being. In fact, your presence here today tells me the man should be locked up and the key swallowed by a fast-slithering rattlesnake."

"For the last time, *what are you talking about?*"

"Rumor has it..." Andrea sighed and sat behind her desk. "No, it isn't rumor. I checked it out and it's fact. Damn it, Jordan. I'm so sorry. Your uncle sold out to the Thorsens."

"What?" Jordan laughed, relaxing back into the chair. "You're wrong. Uncle Cletus would never sell out. Never. Not in a month of Sundays. Not in a million years. Not for a million..." Bucks. The words struck a chord of memory and her laughter died away.

She pictured Rainer in her living room—intent on working at Cornucopia—and bribing Uncle Cletus in order to do it. Rainer had held out that money like a carrot to a jack— She broke off the thought, uncomfortable with the image. He'd held out that money like a succulent morsel of meat to a hungry man. With the bath they'd taken over the ad and the sharp reduction in her uncle's retirement savings, he'd be more than hungry. Uncle Cletus would be starving.

And Rainer knew it.

"Are you listening to me? Jordan!" Andrea's expression reflected her concern. "Are you all right?"

"Are you sure?" Jordan asked in a shaken voice. "There's absolutely no mistake?"

A mist of tears glittered in Andrea's eyes. "I'm sorry," she whispered. "I've checked it from hell to breakfast. It's fact."

Jordan no longer tried to deny the truth of her friend's claim. How could she when it was a sure thing?

Rainer had gone behind her back and bought out Cornucopia.

"He knew, Andrea," she said in a low voice. "He knew we'd be hurting, and he used that information to get at Uncle Cletus."

"You mean because Dad revoked your line of credit?" her friend asked hesitantly.

It took several seconds for her words to sink in. Jordan sat and stared, wondering if she was the only one in the entire universe who knew less than nothing about what was going on. She cleared her throat. "We lost our line of credit, as well?"

Andrea groaned. "You hadn't heard? Cletus didn't mention that, either? Dad called him to discuss it, I'm sure he did."

"Did Rainer know?" Jordan asked tautly.

"Yes. He tried to talk Dad out of—"

"And I thought he cared," Jordan interrupted, her hands balling into fists. "What a fool I've been! I thought we—*I*— meant something to him. But all the time he only cared about getting Cornucopia."

It was a bitter pill to swallow. Just as Seth used her to get free produce, Rainer used her to get the store. Why else would he have kept her buried eyeball-deep in a romantic fog? So he'd have time to accomplish the dastardly deed, that's why!

With an impatient gesture, Andrea shoved a stack of invoices to one side, sheets of white paper forming a blizzard around her desk. "Wait a minute. Your uncle went to Rainer, not the other way around. Rainer had nothing to do with Cletus's decision."

Fury welled inside her. "He had everything to do with it! He knew about our financial setback. He knew we'd lost our line of credit. And he knew it would be the perfect time to put the screws to Uncle Cletus. He even warned me!" She laughed harshly. "He told me everything would be settled by Monday. How right he was."

"You love him, don't you?" Andrea said in astonishment.

Jordan stared at her friend in stony silence, refusing to respond.

"You don't have to answer—your expression says it all." Andrea came over and stooped by Jordan's chair. "Listen, I'm no fan of the Thorsens or their methods. But I'd be careful if I were you. Don't jump to conclusions. Go talk to Rainer. See what he has to say."

"You bet I'm going to see him." She stood up. "And he won't be the only one with something to say."

Andrea grabbed her arm. "Wait! Don't rush into anything. Calm down first."

Jordan shook her head. She'd resigned herself to losing Cornucopia—at least she'd resigned herself to the strong *possibility* of losing it. But Rainer's duplicity was another matter altogether.

Didn't he care how his actions affected her? Had he given her even one moment's consideration? No. And why should he when all he ever wanted was the store? She'd known that from the beginning. Love might have hit her on the head leaving behind a walloping case of romance-induced amnesia, but a brick labeled Indisputable Facts had cured that. And how.

"I have to know the truth," she told Andrea. "I have to see his face and look into his eyes and hear him tell me why he stole my store." She bit hard on her lip. The only problem was she strongly suspected she already knew the answer to that one.

IT TOOK HER three hours to track down Rainer. Three hours of, "You've just missed him—try Thorsen's East." Or West, or South. Would Cornucopia's new name be Thorsen's North? It left a bitter taste in her mouth.

Brita finally found him. "He's at the home office," she told Jordan. "Do you know where that is?"

Without saying a word, Jordan shook her head.

"It's downtown. Here, I'll give you directions." Brita jotted them down and handed over the paper. "Listen, I know it's none of my business, but don't be too rough on him. He—" She stopped abruptly, something in Jordan's expression cutting off whatever she intended to say. "He's expecting you," she said, her tone carrying a defensive edge.

If her words were meant to frighten, they failed. Nothing seemed to penetrate the shell Jordan had built around her feelings. She felt frozen, as if she was only going through the motions. Even her fury was a cold thing, burning like black ice in her heart.

It took forty minutes to find the building, a huge market, standing three stories high—twice the size of Cornucopia. The sign above it read simply Thorsen's. The offices were on the second and third floors, Brita had told her, with Rainer and his brother occupying the third.

Jordan parked her truck and entered the building, expending some of her tension by taking the stairs. Walking down a long hallway, she came to a receptionist's desk. The woman looked up and smiled.

"May I help you?"

"Rainer Thorsen, please," Jordan said in a low voice.

"And your name?"

"Roberts. Jordan Roberts."

There was a brief pause. Then the receptionist offered her another, more forced smile. "Of course, Ms. Roberts. Mr. Thorsen is expecting you. His office is down the hall to the right."

Jordan walked the length of the hall, her heart pounding, her palms damp. She stopped in front of his closed door and wiped her hands on her jeans. Unable to help herself, she reached up to touch her tomato charm, trying to draw comfort from it. Then she released it and closed her hand into a fist. Taking a deep breath, she knocked.

The door opened. Rainer stood there—more formidable than she'd ever seen him—wearing a suit, a tie and his Viking expression.

"Come in, Valkyrie," he said. "I've been expecting you."

CHAPTER TEN

SHE KNEW he'd been expecting her. So why did she feel so intimidated? Jordan swallowed. For whatever reason, she did, and it took every ounce of willpower not to crumble at his feet. All morning, she'd carried her anger like a torch. So where was it? Sputtering, that's where, her wrathful flame dying to a pitiful flicker.

Not giving herself time to think she lifted her chin and stepped over the threshold and into his office. Glancing at Rainer, her banked anger flared anew. Everything about him—his expensive suit, his cool, commanding expression, even that lightning-bolt earring—warned that she was dealing with incredible strength and fierce determination.

On her initial assessment, she'd known what he was: a Viking, a ruthless marauder who took what he wanted. She'd thought he wanted her, but he'd taken Cornucopia. She'd been a fool to think it would end any other way. *If it looks like a rose, has thorns like a rose and smells like a rose, it's bound to have a bee there somewhere,* she thought. And boy, had she been stung.

"I assume you heard about the sale," he said, breaking the silence.

"Oh, I heard, you double-dealing, two-faced son of a—"

"Am I to assume you're not pleased?"

Her breath caught in disbelief. "Not pleased? You mean not pleased that you went behind my back and bought out my store?"

"Your uncle's store."

"Not pleased that you didn't think to include me in the negotiations?"

He shrugged. "You weren't the owner."

"Or not pleased that you didn't care enough about our...our...relationship to even discuss..." Her voice broke despite her best efforts and she glared impotently.

"Why don't we cut to the bottom line and skip the rest," he suggested, and hauled her in' ; arms. "This is all that matters."

Then he kissed her, his mouth firm and determined. And she kissed him right back. It was anger, she tried to convince herself. She was using him, just as he used her. But deep down she knew differently.

She loved this man. And just for a minute she'd pretend he returned her love.

Their embrace lasted forever and a second. She released all her pent-up anger and frustration, all her loneliness and fear, all her love and desire. And he replaced it with a gentle warmth that shattered her defenses. There was a tenderness in his touch that eased the ache within her. The words he murmured into her mouth nourished her body and soul, and his strength became hers.

He thrust his hands into the braid confining her hair, pulling at it, loosening it, so that the dark curls tumbled wildly about her face.

"Now I see the volcano," he muttered, nipping at her lips. "You're an explosion waiting to happen—all heat and fire and fury."

She tightened her hands about his neck, pulling his mouth back to hers. She kissed him deeply, hungrily, angry once again. She'd make him sorry he ever put Cornucopia ahead of her. He might not love her, but he'd remember her. And regret.

"I want you, Jordan. I want you here, and I want you now."

She used the strength he'd given her and stepped back, the frantic ache within her surpassing anything she'd ever experienced. It hurt even to speak. "You have what you want," she managed to say. "You have Cornucopia. Now give me what I want. An explanation."

He shook his head as though to clear it. The passion drained from his face, his expression turning wary. Shadows appeared in his eyes, the intense green stormy and impatient. "Ask your uncle," he said, and folded his arms across his chest, his stance rock solid and defiant.

Jordan stiffened. "I don't have to. I already know. You used insider information. You told Nick about our financial setback, didn't you? As a result we lost our line of credit at Constantine's. You romanced me to keep me quiet, and then when the time was ripe, you moved in for the kill. You went to Uncle Cletus and offered him enough money for Cornucopia that he wouldn't have to worry about money problems ever again."

Rainer reached out and cupped her chin with his hand, forcing her face up. Their eyes met and locked. "Knowing me as you do, you can say such a thing—believe such a thing? You think I'd fake my feelings for you, that I'd try to romance the store out from under you?"

No! she wanted to shout. *I don't believe it!* "Yes!" The word tumbled out of her mouth. She could read the disappointment and pain in his expression. Then there was no expression.

Take it back before it's too late, a part of her cried. But she couldn't. She knew her uncle, her only family in the whole world, wouldn't betray her like that. She had to take her uncle's side, defend him and protect him no matter what the cost. And this time the cost was very, very high.

"So be it." His hand dropped away. "I can't fight your love for your uncle, and I wouldn't do anything to destroy it. But talk to him about it, Jordan. When you do, don't let your loyalty blind you to the truth—and don't let him break your heart."

She stared up at him, a shimmer of tears blurring her vision. *Too late,* she wanted to say. Her heart was already broken. But not by Uncle Cletus, and not by some store. A fierce green-eyed Viking had accomplished that job.

Their discussion was over. She turned and left the office, closing the door softly behind her, knowing she'd just closed it on her future, as well as on her past.

She practically ran down the hallway, tears blinding her. She kept her head lowered as she passed the receptionist, hoping to escape the woman's notice. But the way to the stairs seemed incredibly long. Reaching the end of the hall, she realized she'd taken a wrong turn.

Darn it all! She swiped at her eyes with the back of her hand. Just what she needed—to be caught wandering the halls of Thorsen's sobbing her eyes out.

A door opened beside her. To her fury and frustration, Thor stepped out. He took one look, gripped her elbow and pulled her, protesting all the way, into his office. He reached into his pocket and tugged out a handkerchief, offering it to her.

"Stop arguing and use this," he ordered briskly. "I assume you tried to give Rainer a hard time and came away the worse for wear."

"In your dreams," she muttered rudely.

"No doubt. However, I'm not the one in love with you. Rainer is. Just as you're in love with him." He waited for his words to sink in, then cut cleanly across her objections. "Don't bother to debate the issue. There's nothing to debate—about that."

Her mouth settled into a stubborn line. "I'm not discussing Cornucopia or Uncle Cletus with you."

He lifted a single tawny eyebrow. "Wrong again." He pushed her into a chair and settled onto the edge of his desk, staring down at her. "You refuse to face facts, Ms. Roberts. Perhaps it's a character flaw on your part. I don't know. But this is one fact you *must* face. Your uncle is not a businessman, and therefore he shouldn't attempt to run a business."

"Thanks to you, he doesn't," she couldn't resist pointing out.

He continued as though she hadn't spoken. "As for you, Cornucopia cannot be and should not be a substitute for love or for a family—or for life."

"It's not a substitute, it's a representation of those things," Jordan disputed without conviction. How could she argue with him when he was repeating the very same conclusions she'd drawn the day before?

"It's a business," he contradicted firmly. "That's all. And there's life beyond business." An actual smile touched his broad mouth. "Even I know that."

The fight went out of her and she stared at him, nonplussed. Why had Andrea ever let this man escape? It could only have been temporary insanity. "You're right," she conceded with a sigh.

He reached out and touched the hand that held his balled-up handkerchief. "Then don't sacrifice your life for Cornucopia. It's not worth it."

She stood up. "Anything else?"

He studied her for a moment longer, then his smile turned gentle. "No," he said at last. Rising, he walked her to the door. "I'll escort you to the elevator."

She didn't protest, she knew futile when she saw it. They waited in silence for the elevator. Then Jordan stepped in, jabbing at the first-floor button. The doors started to slide closed, but Thor stopped them at the last minute, holding them open with his hand.

"There's nothing you can do to change what's happened," he said. "But you don't have to lose both Cornucopia and Rainer. He's not responsible for your situation." He removed his hand from the elevator door. "Your uncle is. Talk to him."

IN THE TRUCK on the way home, she mulled over Thor's words. She also thought about her conversation with Rainer. One thing came home loud and clear. Cornucopia wasn't hers. It never had been. As much as that fact hurt, the time had come to face up to it.

Uncle Cletus had sold out. And only he could tell her why.

She slowed as she passed Cornucopia. The store sat in darkness, a large sign on the door proclaiming a grand re-opening scheduled for the following week. Her lips tightened. The Thorsens worked fast.

Parking the truck in front of the house, she hopped out and ran up the steps of the porch, shoving open the front door. "Uncle Cletus!" she called. "Where are you?"

"In here," came the muffled response.

Jordan stepped into the darkened living room, frowning in concern. She flicked on the overhead light. Uncle Cletus sat in his favorite chair, the checkerboard in front of him set up with nectarines and plums. He'd half eaten one of his men.

"Why are you sitting here like this?"

"You know, don't you," he said quietly, "that I sold Cornucopia."

Jordan crossed the room to his side and knelt down by his chair. "Yes, I know." She picked up his gnarled hand, squeezing it gently. "Tell me about it, Uncle Cletus. Tell me why you sold."

"I had to." She heard the plea in his words, and the gray eyes he turned on her were dark and sad. "You have to believe me, girl. I didn't have a choice."

"I believe you." And she did. "Tell me about it."

"It...it has to do with your father," he began. He glanced at her hesitantly. "And the...the accident."

Jordan froze, not anticipating such a response. What could her father's death have to do with the Thorsens? "What are you talking about, Uncle Cletus?"

"It was my fault, you know—your father's death."

"The brakes failed," Jordan said painfully, "and the truck rolled back on him. How could that be your fault?"

He waved a trembling hand in the air. "Oh, I might not have caused the actual accident. But if I'd been better equipped to deal with the store, if I'd been of more help to your father instead of a hindrance, the accident never would have happened." He slumped in the chair and closed his eyes. "Maybe he'd have taken the time to check the brakes if I'd pulled my own weight."

"Uncle Cletus, that's just idle speculation. You can't blame yourself, not for that." Her hand tightened on his. "I certainly don't. You've done so much for me. You've raised me, cared for me, loved me as though I were your own. We're family."

He shook his head. "I owed it to you, and then some. I've been a selfish old man. After the mistake with the ad, I saw history repeating itself, only with you this time, instead of your father."

"I don't understand," she said, puzzled. "This has happened before?"

"Not the ad. No." He shifted in his chair. "I'd come to depend on you more and more. You put so much of yourself into Cornucopia—just like your father and my father before him. What if something happened to you? What if, because of my incompetence, something worse happened than my misjudging some silly ad? I couldn't live with myself if it did."

"That's why you sold out?" she demanded, unable to keep the incredulous note from her voice.

"Not just that." His face puckered in frustration. "I probably would have kept rationalizing everything—allowing you to continue to do most of the work—if it hadn't been for Rainer. Because of him, I saw what I had to do. It only made sense."

Here it comes. Jordan looked away. Now she'd hear how Rainer convinced her uncle to sell. What combination of words had he used to persuade a vulnerable old man to give up his livelihood?

She drew herself up short. Is that what she honestly believed? That Rainer would do something so unethical? So...so despicable?

No. She shook her head automatically. Not in this life or the next. She'd never been more certain of anything. Why hadn't she realized it sooner? If Rainer wanted something, he went after it head-on. He confronted, demanded and—ten times out of ten—received. He didn't sneak behind people's backs. He didn't con old men. *And he didn't romance women in order to get it.*

So, what the devil had Rainer said to her uncle?

"Uncle Cletus," Jordan said in a stern voice, staring him square in the eye, "you and I need to talk turkey. Cornucopia is yours to do with as you will. If that means selling, so be it. It's your choice and I support that choice."

He looked at her in relief. "Do you really mean that?"

"I do." With ruthless disregard, she shoved aside the twinge of regret that thoughts of losing the store generated. "You should also know that I never have and I never will blame you for my father's accident. You've been a vital part of Cornucopia, whether you recognize that fact or not. Without you, it wouldn't have existed."

"But the Thorsens. They'll keep Cornucopia going."

Jordan laughed in genuine amusement. "Maybe. After a fashion. But as you've said, Cornucopia is nothing without a Roberts at the helm. They'll find that out soon enough." And when they did, she'd be right there to pitch in—if they'd allow it.

Her uncle looked utterly confused. "But you and Rainer—"

"Yes, let's discuss Rainer. How the hell did he convince you to sell?"

"Tut-tut," her uncle murmured. "Language, my dear." At her impatient glare he said in a reasonable voice, "He didn't precisely convince me. I decided I'd better sell once I realized you and Rainer were getting married. I know nothing's been officially announced, but I do have eyes. Even Walker noticed. And for him to notice anything that doesn't pop up out of the earth or get picked off a tree or bush... well!"

"What do you mean Rainer and I are getting married?" she cut in, determined to bring him back to that most important point.

He gave her a reproving look. "I'm a traditional man. Rainer's father, Alaric, is a traditional man. At least he was when I knew him. And I'm sure Alaric's sons are also traditional men. Traditional men do not roll around in the grass without . . . without there being a traditional reason.''

Try lust, she almost said aloud. "You mean marriage," she said instead.

"Exactly! Marriage. And since you and Rainer will get married, I had to act." He gave an abashed shrug. "Listen, my dear, I wouldn't know how to tighten a belt, even if I wore one. Once Andrea told Nick about our little money problem—"

"Andrea told Nick about that?" Jordan exclaimed in disbelief.

"Nick called me. Apologized. Said he'd given her a hard time about selling us produce at cost. But once he heard about our problem, he said he'd be delighted to help out. Unfortunately he needed us to pay with cash from now on, same as everybody else.''

"Naturally," she said dryly. And she'd blamed Rainer. Maybe if she'd discussed things more thoroughly with Andrea, she wouldn't have jumped to the wrong conclusion.

"Anyway," Cletus continued, "I'll be danged if I'm going to leave Cornucopia to you without getting so much as a chicken ranch out of it. Because when you marry Rainer, that's precisely what will happen. The Thorsens will get their hands on Cornucopia for nothing, and I won't get to retire to New Mexico with my chickens.''

"Arizona," she reminded him, acknowledging the element of twisted logic in his reasoning.

"Exactly."

Dear sweet Uncle Cletus—ever the optimist. Once things might have worked out the way he thought, but not now. Now she'd be lucky if Rainer ever spoke to her again. She forced a smile to her lips. "I understand why you sold, and you're right. You deserve your chicken ranch.''

"You don't think it's dishonest?" he asked a shade nervously. "The Thorsens can spare the money and then some."

"It's not dishonest," she reassured him. "It's good sound business." And wouldn't Thor laugh himself silly if he heard.

"Then . . . then you're not mad at me?"

She threw her arms around her uncle's neck and gave him a fierce hug. "How could I ever be mad at you? We're family."

And it was the truth.

MUCH LATER she wandered through Cornucopia, unable to resist saying a final farewell to the family market. She ran a hand over the trestled tabletops, frowning at a small jagged tear in the gingham skirt. She'd have to fix that. She caught herself. No, the Thorsens would have to fix that. It wasn't her concern any longer.

What changes would they make? she wondered, looking around. Not the kids corner. Rainer knew how important that was. And the family pictures . . . She crossed the room and stood in front of fifty years' worth of memories. She'd always planned, when she owned Cornucopia, to have her picture taken and hung beside all the others. It hurt, knowing it would never happen. It hurt a lot.

But she'd come to realize she could let go of Cornucopia. With regret, true, but she'd survive. What she couldn't survive was losing Rainer. She'd probably ruined any possibility of a relationship with him by being unable to give him the faith she'd given her uncle. He had it now, but was it too late?

Perhaps not. She frowned. There had to be a workable resolution. An angle. There had to be an angle. If only she could figure out what would work best. She sighed, her shoulders sagging a little. No angle, she realized. The time for angles was past. She stuck a hand in her right pocket, her fingers closing around her double-headed nickel. It would take more than a coin toss to pull this one off.

She stopped in her tracks. Or would it? Perhaps she had one angle left after all.

IT TOOK HER LESS than thirty minutes to drive back to Thorsen's home office. She parked, then raced down the sidewalk, up the three flights of stairs and past the startled receptionist to Rainer's office. She pounded on his door.

"He's not there," Thor said from behind her.

She turned. "Where is he?"

"Why should I tell you?"

Jordan advanced on him. "I'll go around you, through you, even under you if I have to. I'll search this market and every other Thorsen market until I find him. And I won't be quiet about it, either. That man has met his match and I'm here to let him know it."

His lips twitched. "Ah, the Valkyrie has awakened—at last. Have you come to sweep the warrior of your choice off to Valhalla?"

"To Valhalla, Walla Walla or Timbuktu. Do you move, or do I move you?"

Without another word, he stepped to one side, waiting until she'd passed him before adding, "He's downstairs. And fair warning, warrior maiden—" she glanced back at him "—he's angry."

Angry. Fine. At least he wasn't indifferent. Angry meant he cared. Angry she could handle. Maybe.

She saw him the moment she entered the store. The number of customers and the hectic pace of business amazed her, but through all the confusion, she instantly zeroed in on Rainer.

He was back in his jeans and T-shirt, laboring harder and faster than anyone around. His muscles rippled, a faint film of perspiration evident beneath the thin cotton shirt. Shaking her head, she watched as he swung a hundred-pound sack of potatoes onto his shoulder and carried it out to the spud rack. It reminded Jordan of her grandfather, and she experienced the same awe, mixed with a sharp sense of pride.

And desire.

This was *her* man. Now to convince Rainer of that fact.

She caught up with him by the tomato display. He didn't turn at her approach, but she saw the muscles in his back stiffen.

"What do you want?" he snapped, not pausing a beat as he yanked the wooden slats off the top of a tomato crate.

"I was wrong, you were right, and I'm sorry."

"So I'm not the bad guy anymore, is that it?" He glanced at her then, and she nearly flinched at the coldness of his gaze. "You toss out a quick apology and that makes everything all right?"

"No, not all right. But it's a place for us to start, a place to go on from."

He gave a short humorless laugh. "You're taking a lot for granted."

She pushed down her alarm, refusing to show the doubt and uncertainty surging through her. Did he love her? Perhaps she had assumed too much. Either way, it didn't matter. She loved him, and she'd risk everything on that fact alone. "You won't get rid of me that easily," she warned.

He shot her a fierce look. "Because of Cornucopia, you mean? It all comes back to that, doesn't it?"

"Forget Cornucopia! I don't care about Cornucopia."

He dumped the tomatoes into the bin with careless disregard. "Yeah. Right. Now tell me something I can believe."

She balled her hands into fists, refusing to give up. "I didn't come back because of the store. I came back because you need me in your life. And I need you in mine." She gazed at him, willing him to hear the sincerity in her voice. "Darn it, Rainer. I love you." She reached inside her shirt and pulled out the tomato charm hanging around her neck. "Do I keep this, or do I return it? Do you love me, or not?"

Fury exploded deep in his eyes—the green hard and clear as splintered glass. With a muffled oath, he reached down and grabbed her around the waist. "Love you? You don't care about love. This is just an excuse to get your hands on that damned market. Well, here's what you can do with Cornucopia," he said. He picked her up, dropping her down onto the display of ripe juicy *Lycopersicon esculentum*. "Make love to that."

Tomatoes burst beneath her, the warm juice oozing up around her. The rich fragrance of *L'air du Tomate* wafted between them. In truth, she was afraid to move. Wide-eyed she stared at the man she loved, knowing she had to act—knowing it was now or never.

Ignoring the horrified gasps from the nearby customers, ignoring the sticky wetness spreading beneath her and ignoring her somewhat tacky position, she grabbed the front of Rainer's shirt and hung on for dear life. "You haven't answered my question," she announced in a loud clear voice.

"What question?"

"Do you love me?"

He glared down at her. "Why should I answer that? How do I know you don't want me because I own Cornucopia?"

He threw her own words back at her. "How do I know you're not romancing me for my store?"

He'd turned the tables on her fair and square. She took a deep breath, praying her only remaining angle would work. "You don't. You'll have to trust me . . . or . . . or we can flip a coin and settle it once and for all." She held her breath, nerves transforming her stomach into a toxic wasteland.

His eyes narrowed. "What do you mean?"

Jordan leaned back and shoved her hand into her left pocket, squashed tomatoes sticking to her shirt. She yanked out her nickel.

"We're going to settle our problems with a double-sided coin again?" he said scornfully. "That won't solve a thing. All I have to do is pick heads and I win."

"Trust, remember? You asked me for trust, and now I'm asking it of you. Heads, I want you for Cornucopia. Tails I want you because I love you." With a quick flick of her thumbnail, she sent the coin spinning high above them.

Rainer caught it midspin. "Tails," he said, white-faced, the coin buried in his fist. "It's tails."

"Look at it," Jordan whispered. "Look."

Slowly his hand unclenched and he stared down at the coin.

"It doesn't matter which side comes up," she whispered. "It's all the same. I love *you*, not Cornucopia."

He hesitated for a long minute, then carefully turned the nickel over. In the next instant he'd swept her into his arms—tomatoes and all—the double-tailed coin tumbling heedlessly to the ground.

"I love you, Jordan Roberts," he declared for all the world to hear. "You are my life and my love. I want you by my side for the rest of our days on this earth. What do you have to say about that?"

She laughed, running her hands up the sides of his face, her fingers lingering on his lightning-bolt earring. "Haven't you told me over and over again that you always get what you want? Well, Viking, now you have me. Are you going to make an honest woman of me, or will I need to bribe you with a love apple?"

He buried his hands in her dark hair. "Bribe me now, Valkyrie. Then you'll have to marry me."

That said, he lowered his head and kissed her, hoisting her out of the tomato bin. Squashed tomatoes plopped to the floor at their feet, a stream of red juice puddling around them.

Throughout the store, the customers cheered and went back to their shopping with happy smiles—all except one portly old man.

"Hmph!" he muttered. "If they think I'm paying thirty-nine cents a pound for *those* tomatoes, they'd better think again!"

EPILOGUE

"WE DON'T HAVE much longer, Mrs. Thorsen," the photographer announced, glancing up at the darkening September sky. "If we don't get this shot taken soon, the light will be all wrong."

Jordan's brows drew together. She'd waited a lot of years for this day to arrive, and she didn't want anything to spoil it. "Give it one more minute. I'm sure they'll be right out." She stood by the market entrance. "Hurry up in there!"

Rainer joined her. "Take it easy love. We're coming."

She shifted impatiently. "You know how important this picture is to me. I want it to be perfect."

"Yes, Valkyrie. I do know," he said, and kissed her.

As she did every time he used that particular method of calming her, Jordan relaxed against him, the tension draining away. A tiny satisfied smile spread across her mouth, even as color darkened her cheeks.

She'd never been happier than during the past twelve months. Tomorrow would be their first anniversary. Tears misted her eyes. Day by day their lives melded and solidified as their love and happiness gained in strength.

Rainer touched her cheek with a gentle finger. "You cry a lot. It worries me."

"Don't let it." She snuggled against him and grasped her tomato charm in a now familiar gesture. "You know it's from happiness."

The photographer cleared his throat. "Mrs. Thorsen' You about ready?"

She sighed. "Almost—I think. We'll want our new sig in the photo. Can you do that?"

"No problem." He glanced up at the bright white-and green placard. "'Cornucopia I,' huh? You guys must b expanding."

Rainer grinned proudly. "Sure are." He winked at hi wife. "And in more ways than one, come the end of nex month."

Jordan lifted her chin. "Tomorrow Cornucopia III open farther north, in Lake City," she announced. "Of course i can't compare to the original."

Rainer's hold tightened. "Nothing can compare to that,' he murmured.

The photographer frowned. "The light's almost gone. W can't wait any longer."

"Where's Uncle Cletus?" Jordan muttered anxiously "We can't take the picture without him."

Right on cue her uncle appeared in the doorway. "I'n coming. I'm coming. What's all the rhubarb? Can't an old man have a quiet game of checkers without these interruptions. I should have retired to my chicken ranch in New Mexico like I wanted, instead of letting you talk me out of it."

"Arizona, Uncle Cletus," Jordan and Rainer corrected in unison.

Cletus snorted. "Whatever. I was winning, you know. Three more moves and I'd have done it."

"Six," came the grumbling retort. Walker poked his head out from behind Cletus, a pineapple in one hand, an eggplant in the other. He looked at Jordan. "Me, too?" he asked in a hopeful voice.

Before Uncle Cletus could say a word, Jordan took Walker firmly by the arm and pulled him into the warmth of their circle. "You, too," she said. "This picture is history. And history has to be accurate. Which means it's going to have *all* the family." She laid a gentle hand on her well-rounded stomach, smiling with satisfaction and a deep happy contentment. "And with any luck, we'll soon need a bigger picture wall. A *much* bigger wall."

Andrea Constantine and Thor Thorsen—
will they ever make a match of it?
Watch for Day Leclaire's next Harlequin Romance,
A WHOLESALE ARRANGEMENT.

Following the success of WITH THIS RING,
Harlequin cordially invites you to enjoy the
romance of the wedding season with

BARBARA BRETTON
RITA CLAY ESTRADA
SANDRA JAMES
DEBBIE MACOMBER

A collection of romantic stories that celebrate the joy,
excitement, and mishaps of planning that special day
by these four award-winning Harlequin authors.

**Available in April at your favorite Harlequin
retail outlets.**